SNOWFALL

Suzanne Cass

S C
STORM CLOUD
PRESS

Snowfall

Storm Cloud Press, Perth Australia

Copyright © 2021 by Suzanne Cass

Edits by Tanya Saari

Cover by Vikncharlie

All rights reserved.

To Gary, my Big Sky Love.

CHAPTER ONE

Stella Pereira stomped out of the kitchen storeroom and slammed her phone down on the large, oak table. She gritted her teeth and looked up at the ceiling to stop herself from screaming. Ooh, her mother was so infuriating, Stella wanted to kick something. Luckily, there was no one around to see her fit of temper; the kitchen was empty for a change. Even Joseph and Violet were in the foyer, enjoying a glass of bubbly with the rest of the staff. She'd been hiding in the storeroom for some privacy while she'd made her call. Now, she should go out and join the party. And she would...just as soon as she got her temper back under control.

Pulling out one of the many wooden chairs around the table, she sat down with a heavy sigh. That little internal voice had warned her not to call her mother, and she should've listened to it. Her New Year's Eve was practically ruined. Part of her always knew the call was going to end with her mother's stony goodbye, not even wishing her a happy New Year before she hung up, leaving Stella feeling like the unsatisfactory daughter who could never please her mother, no matter how hard she tried. Juliette was not happy that her daughter was spending Christmas—and now New Year's—in America, rather than back in France.

Auntie Celeste would understand. Perhaps she would call her tonight and wish her a happy New Year, then cry on her shoulder. She would help Stella feel better; tell her that Juliette had her own internal demons to deal with, and to try not to take her constant criticism to heart.

Stella's phone vibrated on the table. When she turned it over, another heavy sigh left her lips. To make her evening worse, Armand, her fiancé, was now dodging her calls, sending her texts all day, instead. The message read:

It's time you came back to France. You're wasting your precious skills as a pastry chef working on that godforsaken ranch in the middle of nowhere. Come home, now.

The screen glowed ghostly green in the semidarkness of the kitchen, and Stella fought the urge to put her head in her hands and cry. But it was New Year's Eve. A significant night for Stargazer Ranch. The day after tomorrow, they would re-open to the public after six months spent rebuilding parts of the lodge that'd burnt down in an arson attack perpetrated by two brothers. Cyrus was the older bother of Alex, who'd once been an ex-employee at the ranch, and now they were both spending the next twenty years in prison for their crimes.

Stella had been a victim of one of those fires Cyrus had lit in an attempt to ruin Dean, the ranch's owner. She'd been trapped in the ranch's home-built observatory when the arsonist had locked them all in and set fire to the building. Even now, she had a healthy appreciation for fresh air and unconfined places. And she still suffered bad dreams, but she was determined not to let them get to her. She was stronger than that pathetic man who'd tried to burn them all alive. She was taking a leaf out of Dean's book. Dean hadn't let the horrible events break him. And now he was making plans to rebuild the observatory. He said it was a chance to make it bigger and better.

While Dean was rebuilding, most of the staff had used the

enforced break to go home and visit their respective families. Stella had used her time to travel around this vast country of America, instead. Her mother would've never let her hear the end of it, if she knew Stella had chosen not to go home. So, Stella downplayed the whole thing, not telling anyone back home what'd really happened. And she hadn't had to go far to see so many amazing things for her to wonder at. The Grand Canyon had been her favorite. Then there was Old Faithful geyser in Yellowstone National Park. And watching intrepid climbers scale the cliff face of El Capitan in Yosemite. They had been her top three.

But Montana was just as beautiful, with it's amazing Bitterroot Mountains, so, she'd been more than happy to come back nearly a month before the rest of the staff, to help Joseph, and their newly hired casual help, Violet, re-stock the kitchen, and make sure it was running smoothly before the guests returned.

Stella stood, determined not to let tonight be a total write-off. Marching down the hallway, she pushed open the door to the grand foyer, the heart of the Stargazer lodge. Warmth and noise and light hit her with a rush as she walked through. A large fire was blazing in the biggest fireplace she'd ever seen, and flagstone floors set off the huge, rustic, wooden beams. There must've been at least thirty people milling around the foyer, gathered in small groups, chatting. The vaulted ceiling soared up nearly two floors, large glass panels at the top allowing a spectacular view of the night sky. Strings of party lights zig-zagged across the room, providing a subtle glow, and some leftover Christmas decorations made the place feel cozy. This room never ceased to amaze Stella. Actually, this entire building was amazing. Dean and Naomi had turned this log cabin into one of the most beautiful and tasteful lodges she'd ever seen. If the foyer was the heart of the lodge, then the lodge was the heart of their ranch-style, boutique resort.

One of the new wait staff, Roxanne, passed in front of Stella, carrying a sliver tray and she snagged a glass of bubbly, giving the other girl a smile. She finally spotted Penny, her best friend, talking to Emily and Tom on the other side of the room.

"Hello." The greeting came from behind her left shoulder, just as she took a step in Penny's direction. The voice was familiar and sent a shiver down her spine.

Wyatt Wilson.

That gravelly tone was embedded in her psyche from their night spent snowbound in his pickup truck a week ago.

She hadn't noticed him as she entered the room, because as usual, Wyatt was standing at the back of the crowd, drinking beer and watching as everyone else partied. This time, when she looked at him, Wyatt didn't avert his gaze, as he so often did. She liked that she had to tilt her head up slightly to look him in the face. She was tall, nearly five foot eleven—her Aunt Celeste used to joke she should've been a model, not a pastry chef—and that meant a lot of men were shorter than her. Not Wyatt, however.

"Hello," she repeated. *Zut*, did she just sound more like a startled mouse than a self-assured woman? She tried again. "Good to see you." She raised her glass, and he clinked his bottle against it. Yep, that time her voice sounded much more composed and smoother. She could do this.

"You, too," he replied. There was a pause as he stared at her.

Wyatt was still a man of few words, it would seem.

"Levi said you weren't coming tonight." If she'd known he was going to be here, she might've prepared herself mentally. As it was, she felt like a gasping fish out of water, not knowing what to say next. Wyatt lived with his brother, Levi, and his fianceé, Cat. Levi had told her yesterday that Wyatt wouldn't make it, and she was glad she wouldn't have to confront her confusing feelings about him. It was probably better if she didn't see too much of him; she had Armand, after all.

But try telling that to her body; her skin prickled with awareness at his proximity, and her heart did a strange thudding deep inside her chest.

"I guess I changed my mind." Wyatt tipped his head on the side and smiled at her. Oh, wow. Wyatt was the serious type; he rarely smiled. But when he did, it lit up the room, along with her insides. She remembered the first time she'd seen him smile. It was after he'd rescued her from the crashed truck. He'd helped her up the ravine, and they'd had to shelter from the enormous blizzard engulfing the Bitterroot Mountains in his truck. They'd waited by the side of the road all night for the storm to blow itself out. She'd learned a lot about Wyatt Wilson that night. She'd learned that talking about cooking made him smile. As did the taste of his mother's pignoli cookies.

"I'm glad you did," she replied. It was true, her feelings might be mixed when it came to Wyatt, but one thing was for certain, she liked his steady, calming influence.

"How's your head?" He reached up a hand, as if to touch the still-healing scar running along her hairline, then thought better of it and dropped it back down by his side.

"It's good. The doctor said you'll hardly be able to see the scar soon." She'd hit her head on the steering wheel when the truck had crashed head-on into a large tree. Wyatt had bandaged it for her and kept her awake, in case of concussion.

"That's great."

There was another awkward silence. Stella didn't know what to say. She'd already thanked Wyatt profusely after he rescued her, and he'd brushed most of her thanks away, as if

5

embarrassed. Surely, she needed to find something else to talk about. If they were to be friends—or whatever it was they were—she had to get over her feeling of indebtedness to him.

But as she stared at him, the image of Wyatt kissing her on Christmas Day overwhelmed her mind. They'd been standing in the doorway of the storeroom. Joseph had strung up bunches of mistletoe, but she hadn't noticed this particular bunch, until now. Stella had heard of the American tradition, but never partaken in it. Wyatt's questing gaze and fixed on her and she'd swallowed hard. His lips had found hers. Warm and weighty, demanding. Her tongue darted out to taste him. His free arm snaked around her waist, jerking her into his chest, almost lifting her feet off the ground. His desire fueled her own, and she tilted her head to get better access to his mouth. He was nothing like any man she'd ever kissed before. He wasn't some tame, domesticated male. With Wyatt, there was an edge to his desire, a dark edge, that he seemed to be barely able to control. She'd liked it.

A hot flush crept up her neck and she shook her head to rid herself of the memory. Out of the corner of her eye, she caught Cat smirking at her through the crowd. The other woman clearly thought there was something going on between her and Wyatt. Seeing Cat, inspiration hit as to her next topic of conversation.

"So, have Cat and Levi set a date yet?"

"What?" He paused, beer bottle halfway to his lips.

"For their wedding. I heard they were going to hold it here, at the ranch."

"Oh, right, that." He gave a one-shoulder shrug and Stella had to hide a smile.

It seemed weddings weren't Wyatt's thing. Cat and Levi had become engaged six months ago, after they both survived a raging wildfire, the first of the arsonist attacks.

Stella liked Cat; she was feisty, with a sharp tongue, but at least you always knew where you stood with her. Cat was the complete opposite to Levi, who was warm and agreeable and easy to be around. Even though they were an odd couple, they seemed to gel together, making a stronger whole.

"Yeah, I think they're planning it for the first day of summer. That'll be exactly a year since they got engaged," Wyatt finally said.

"Oh, that's so sweet." Stella couldn't help it, she knew she was gushing, but it was romantic.

"I guess so." Wyatt looked slightly confused, and she had to quell her urge to roll her eyes. Men, they were all so clueless when it came to romance. Especially American men.

Her phone vibrated in her hand, and without thinking, she tipped it up to see who it was. Armand. Again.

Why are you ignoring me? I need you to tell me you're coming home, or else…

"Problems?" Wyatt must've seen her expression change as she checked her phone, because his black eyes softened slightly. Wyatt didn't know she had a fiancé, unless he'd heard it from someone else, because she hadn't mentioned him. She should've told him after he kissed her on Christmas Day. But the words just wouldn't come.

"No… Yes." She shrugged. How did she explain? Armand was complicated. This whole engagement thing was complicated. And Wyatt—or the way her body reacted to Wyatt—made her feelings about it even more tangled. Stella didn't know if there was anything between her and Wyatt, or even if she wanted there to be anything between them. One thing her mother had taught her—that she actually agreed with—was not to keep secrets.

She squared her shoulders. "I have a boyfriend back in France."

The only sign that Wyatt heard her was a telltale lift of one eyebrow.

"Well, technically, he's my fiancé," she blurted.

"I see." He kept his obsidian gaze fixed on her, but there was a subtle change in his eyes, like a wall had come down inside his mind.

Zut. She'd done it now. Scared him off. Maybe that was for the best.

Before she could say any more, Levi came up and tapped Wyatt on the shoulder. "Hey, bro, sorry to interrupt." He flicked Stella an apologetic smile. "There's some guy over by the door, asking for you."

"What?" Wyatt's head snapped around. "Who is it?"

"Says his name is Tony."

Wyatt followed Levi's gaze toward the front door. A muscled jumped in his jaw as he studied the man.

"Yeah, he's an old friend from..." Wyatt didn't finish his sentence, glancing around to see if anyone had heard him. Stella knew what he'd been about to say. Wyatt had spent two years in prison. Few people knew about his time in lockup. Wyatt didn't like to talk about it, he thought people would think less of him if they knew. This must be a fellow inmate.

Wyatt had been convicted of rape and murder. But he was innocent. And had finally been exonerated. The fact that it'd taken so long for the police to catch the actual killer and the courts to release him, however, had left Wyatt angry and resentful.

"Sorry," Wyatt said. "I'd better go." Stella caught the glimpse of regret in Wyatt's eyes, before he turned to tell his brother he'd see him at home, and put his half-drunk bottle of beer down on the nearest table.

She watched Wyatt's retreating back, following the line of his lovely, broad shoulders, and an unconscious sigh escaped her lips. He was deliciously gorgeous.

But not for her. She had too many other issues to deal with. One of them being an angry fiancé. The other being her indecision on exactly how long she wanted to stay in Montana. Maybe she should go home, like everyone was telling her. Her trip had been unplanned and impulsive. She'd applied for the job as assistant chef on the ranch, never in her wildest dreams thinking she'd get it. Then three days later, as she'd been running late for work at the patisserie, her cell had rung and it'd been Naomi, Dean's wife, on the other end, offering her a job. Stella was a believer in fate. Everything always happened for a reason. Positive thinking was the best way to get through the hurdles life threw at her. So, she'd followed her instincts and moved to Montana. The contract was for a year, but Stella had only been here seven months, so far. There was a lot more she wanted to achieve before she left.

Wyatt met the other man near the front door to the lodge. Tony was tall and wiry, pretty average looking. He was still wearing his down jacket and knit cap from his trek through the snow outside. There was a slight tilt to the man's mouth that Stella didn't like.

Wyatt and the man disappeared through the door, Wyatt grabbing his coat from the rack near the door as he went.

Stella's phone vibrated again.

It was Armand. His text read:

Come back to France now, or I'm ending this sham of an engagement.

CHAPTER TWO

"What are you doing here?" Wyatt snarled, not caring if his blunt question offended the other man.

"I needed to see you. Make sure my…package was safe." Tony lifted a corner of his mouth in a cheeky grin. Back when he first met Tony, Wyatt had seen that smile as a form of friendship. But he knew enough now to distrust it. That grin meant trouble.

"Besides, you weren't that hard to track down. Seems like everyone knows everyone else in these small towns." Tony stopped walking and pulled Wyatt by the elbow, turning him around to face him. "So, is my package safe?"

"What the hell, man? You can't come here and interrupt my New Year's Eve. Everybody inside saw you." Wyatt shook Tony's hand off and glared at him. Levi would kill him if he knew what was going on. He didn't think he could cope with the disappointment that would show on his younger brother's face if he found out. At times, it felt a little like Levi was the older brother. He was certainly acting like it; he had the steady job, a fianceé and was renting a great house. While Wyatt… Well, he didn't have a lot to show for his life so far. And Levi also had an impressive beard, as well. Wyatt was a little jealous of Levi's beard, because he'd never been able to grow a proper one himself. It gave him an air of seriousness that hadn't been there back before Wyatt went into jail. His little brother had definitely grown up.

"So what? That ain't my problem." Tony interrupted his thoughts, the smarmy grin leaving his lips, his features morphing into something harder and much colder.

Not for the first time, Wyatt wished he'd never met Tony. When Wyatt had originally landed in prison, it'd been so disorienting and downright scary, and Tony had been talkative and affable. Wyatt didn't make friends easily, but everyone needed someone to guard their back in prison. For a while, he'd used Tony's company like a security blanket. Tony, too, had only recently been sent to jail, and so both of them found their way through the maze of social etiquette in the prison hierarchy together. They were of a similar age, both celebrating their thirtieth birthday within days of each other. They were interested in some of the same things. NASCAR racing and the Texas Rangers' baseball games were common topics of their conversations.

But it wasn't until Wyatt had known Tony a whole year that he found out Tony had a connection to Dmytro Melink. Dmytro was bad news, and Wyatt wanted nothing to do with him. After that, he saw Tony in a different light.

Wyatt gave a disgusted snort in Tony's direction and walked toward his pickup. "How did you get out here?" Last time Tony had breezed into town, he'd hitchhiked. Wyatt didn't think Tony would've had much chance of hitching a ride out to the ranch in the snow at this time of night. Not on New Year's Eve.

"I borrowed a car."

Wyatt stopped in his tracks again and whipped his head around to stare at Tony. The look on his face said it all. "Shit, man." Wyatt hung his head. Tony had stolen a car. That was the absolute last thing he needed. It was the last thing Tony

Suzanne Cass

needed, too, but the guy didn't seem to have the same need for self-preservation as Wyatt. Either that, or he was desperate. Which, looking at Tony's frown, seemed to be more likely.

"What? I'll take it back where I got it from. Like I said, I borrowed it. There was no other way for me to get out here." Tony's voice had risen to a nasal whine.

"Come on, let's talk in my truck." Wyatt turned, and kept walking toward the parking lot. He wasn't worried someone would overhear them out here, but it'd be much warmer in the cab, out of the icy wind.

Swinging up into the truck, he leaned over and unlocked the passenger door for Tony to get in. Then he started the motor and let it idle, willing it to warm up fast. Tony jumped in, rubbing his hands together.

"Who knew it got so cold in these shitty mountains? Why in hell you wanna live here is beyond me," Tony said.

Wyatt didn't answer; he didn't want to partake in Tony's small talk. Sitting in the pickup brought back memories of him and Stella, snowbound, waiting out the night with a blizzard raging outside the truck, curled together on the bench seat for warmth. They'd talked for many hours, then slept in each other's arms, wrapped in blankets to stay warm. He'd felt a connection, something he hadn't had with another woman for a very long time, not since he'd landed in jail.

"Why couldn't you have waited 'til morning?" He wanted to add—instead of crashing the party—but he implied it in his glare. Wyatt was livid at Tony for turning up tonight. Now, everybody knew about their association. Even if they didn't know who Tony was, it always paid to be careful. But Tony didn't seem to care.

"Nah, couldn't wait. I'm outta here tomorrow. But I need my package."

Wyatt blew out a long exhale. Of course he did. Tony was

12

volatile and unpredictable. A little over a week ago, he'd come to Wyatt, begging him to hide a bag for him. Said that he wanted to keep it out of sight for the next few months. Wyatt had wanted nothing to do with Tony or his bag. But Tony had begged, and eventually Wyatt gave in. Because they'd been buddies in prison. And because they had a relationship forged in the pits of adversity. Wyatt didn't like it, but he owed Tony. There was a debt of honor between them.

Which was perhaps serendipity. Because if Wyatt hadn't been coming back from that old, abandoned house a week ago where he'd hidden the bag, he wouldn't have come across Stella's crashed truck.

"Shit, Tony. Really?" Wyatt put his head in his hands.

"Yeah, really." Tony's voice hardened. "Look, I'm sorry to ruin your New Year's Eve. But I got things I need to do." He paused for a second and Wyatt looked up to see a curl at the edge of Tony's impish grin. "It seemed like you had quite a little party of your own going on with that cute chick in the corner."

Wyatt narrowed his eyes at Tony. "What?" His voice was low and dangerous.

"Yeah, I saw the two of you from the doorway. Having a nice ol' chat, you were."

Wyatt didn't know where Tony was going with this, but he didn't like his tone. A sudden sliver of ice formed in his spine. If he'd put Stella at risk, he'd never forgive himself. And what about Cat and Levi? Were they in any danger, too?

Voice even and his fears kept hidden, Wyatt said, "Well, you're just gonna have to wait. The place I stashed it is hard to get to." The winding road out to the abandoned house would be slippery and dangerous, especially at night. A light dusting of snow was falling, even now. Wyatt wasn't prepared to take the risk of hitting a patch of ice and sliding off the road. "And it'll be impossible to find it in the dark, anyway." It'd taken Wyatt two days to get his pickup cleared from out of the snow after the blizzard. The snowplow hadn't made it up the road until the day after Christmas, and even then, he'd had to ask Levi to help him dig it out of the deep drifts. But he wouldn't have it any other way. Not after rescuing Stella. It'd taken another two days for Dean to organize a towing company to winch the shattered truck Stella had been driving back up to the road. It'd been a write-off, and Dean was still waiting for the Chevy dealer to ship him up his new one.

Tony made an impatient noise, unhappy with Wyatt's decision. Wyatt wondered exactly what was in that backpack Tony had given him. He'd told himself, the less he knew the better, so he resisted the urge to take a peek. Tony had never offered to tell him, and Wyatt wisely decided not to ask.

"There's nothing I can do. You can't just turn up out of the blue and expect me to jump whenever you snap your fingers." Wyatt raised his hands in the air.

"Fine. I'll come past your place at lunchtime tomorrow. Make sure you have it by then."

"No, don't." Wyatt grimaced. He'd like to keep Tony away from his family, if possible. The less time he spent near his house or his loved ones, the better. "Meet me out the back of CJ's Den. The burger place on Main Street. There's a side alley. I'll be out there at midday."

"Sounds good, bro." Tony smiled and reached for the door handle.

"Do you promise to leave me alone after this?"

Tony looked up, surprise showing on his face. "Yeah, yeah, I promise." He pursed his lips "It's good that you're trying to get your life back on track. At least one of us is. I don't wanna mess this up for you. Really, I don't, Wyatt."

Maybe Tony was telling the truth. Maybe somewhere

inside, Tony had a good heart, but his grasp of reality was skewed. He told Wyatt that he wanted to be rid of Dmytro, but Wyatt always wondered how deeply imbedded Tony was in the mob boss's dealings.

"See ya tomorrow. Midday, sharp." With that, Tony got out of the truck and slammed the door. Wyatt watched the wiry man make his way across the parking lot and get into a brand-new Lexus. Shit, the guy was unbelievable. Talk about making a spectacle of himself. Even if Tony returned the car to its rightful owner, there was no way it wouldn't cause a stir in this small town. The taillights disappeared into the trees.

He sat for a while, wondering if he should go back into the party. It was nearly midnight. They'd all be wishing each other Happy New Year, singing "Auld Lang Syne", and kissing each other. Wyatt shivered at the thought of kissing Stella again. Those leaf-green eyes staring up into his face. Up close, her eyes were something else. Clear and luminous, with a slightly darker ring around the iris. He remembered her soft lips from Christmas Day, under the mistletoe. Remembered how pliant and willing she'd been in his arms. The mere notion of it had his cock standing to attention. Perhaps it was better not to go inside, with everything happening with Tony at the moment. And the fact he was an ex-con. It wasn't the right time for him to be having any sort of relationship.

And especially not after Stella had revealed she had a boyfriend. He should've guessed a beautiful woman like her wouldn't be single. He just wished he'd known earlier. Perhaps he wouldn't have made such a fool of himself, kissing her under the mistletoe. And he certainly wouldn't have come to the party tonight.

Still, it was par for the course; women weren't to be trusted; he'd learned that the hard way. The whole reason he'd ended up in prison in the first place was because of a woman. Because he'd been trying to protect a woman. But it'd backfired, big time. She'd ended up dead. And he'd ended up in jail, accused of a crime he didn't commit.

Wyatt slammed the pickup into gear. Was his life is ever going to be normal again? Or was he going to lurch from one screwup to the next? He was trying hard to get back into a regular routine. At least he now had a job, and thanks to Levi, a place to live. On the outside, it probably looked to people like he was slotting back into society. But on the inside, he had to live with the acid resentment eating away at his guts. He was a changed man because of his time spent in prison. And even though it wasn't his fault, he was going to have to live with the stigma of that for the rest of his life.

He drove the old, orange Chevy out of the parking lot, taking care on the winding road. It'd do him no good to take his anger out on his truck; he'd only end up in a ditch, or dead by the side of the road.

Wyatt stilled, the idea sparking a certain interest deep inside him. After only a second or two, Wyatt shrugged that thought away. He wasn't the type to wallow in his own misery. And he'd never do that to Levi and Cat. He just needed to keep moving forward. And that meant taking a drive to the old, ruined house out on Black Pine Ridge Road to retrieve a mysterious package in the morning.

CHAPTER THREE

Two days later, Stella stood next to the outdoor barbecue, the heat emanating from the whole pig turning slowly on the spit roast making her sweat, despite the cool temperatures outside. Stargazer Ranch was finally welcoming back all of its guests. There was an air of excitement, a buzz surrounding the staff. This was what they'd been waiting for. Cars were lining up in the parking lot, and Stella could imagine Naomi and Penny being run off their feet with everyone checking in. Dean would be in his absolute element, receiving every guest individually, his charming smile on show. This was why he'd built this special lodge, so he could share it with everyone.

Stella smiled to herself. Dean was such an extrovert; she could never be like him. But she admired him greatly, and knew she'd been lucky to find him as a boss.

She, Joseph, and Violet had been busy all morning prepping a mountain of food. Joseph had started the spit roast well before dawn, to make sure it was ready on time. Everyone agreed the lodge was now better than before. Joseph had worked with a designer and they'd come up with the perfect new kitchen.

"A new year and a new beginning," Dean liked to say to anyone who'd listen.

"Hi there, Stella. Where do you want this?" She turned around to see Cat and Wyatt struggling toward her, carrying a metal barbecue. She was so shocked at the sight of Wyatt that she completely forgot the question. What was he doing here? She hadn't seen him since he'd gone off with that man, Tony, before midnight on New Year's Eve.

"Stella, this is heavy," Cat grunted. Dean had mentioned something about Joseph needing another barbecue for all the ribs and steaks he had yet to grill.

"Over here," she said, pointing to a cleared section between the spit roast and a large, wooden table.

"Wow, that smells amazing," Cat said, lifting her nose in the barbecue's direction.

"It's one of Joseph's specialties. Along with his secret recipe sauce for his ribs. Are you staying for the food?" Stella was looking at Cat, but watching Wyatt out of the corner of her eye.

"You bet," Cat replied. "Levi's coming, as soon as he can get away from work." Wyatt cast a dark look at his soon-to-be-sister-in-law. She shrugged. "Sorry, bro, didn't I tell you? You're stuck here for the afternoon."

Wyatt looked about to argue, but Cat jumped in first. "C'mon, it's the weekend, lighten up. You don't have to be so serious all the time." Cat disappeared in the direction of the parking lot, not giving him a chance to reply. She was one woman who always spoke her mind. Which Stella generally thought was a good thing. But looking at Wyatt's dark frown, she decided a little diplomacy sometimes worked better.

"Did you have something you needed to get back to town for? A shift at CJ's? I can drive you in, if you like." The words left her tongue before she had time to think. She was stupid to make the offer; there was no way Joseph would let her leave the ranch right now.

But the frown smoothed at her words, and his gaze

softened. "No, I'm not working until tomorrow. Thank you, though. I just didn't expect... Never mind."

Why would anyone pass up free food? Unless it was because of all the people about to descend on the covered area. Wyatt wasn't good with people. An awkward silence fell around them. He was doing that thing again, where he avoided her gaze.

"Can I help with anything else while I'm here?" he asked.

"You could set out those chairs over there." Stella pointed at a stack of folded chairs, leaning against one of the large, upright poles. "Dean was going to send Dale down to do it, but he hasn't appeared."

"Be glad to."

Stella went back to tending the barbecue, keeping track of those broad shoulders as she cooked. Wyatt had on the same black jeans and black sheepskin coat he'd worn the night he rescued her. He pulled a knit cap out of one of his pockets and put it on, covering his shock of black hair. Watching him move, his easy gait as he strode back and forth between the pile of chairs and where he was setting them up, Stella felt something stir low in her belly. He was tall and lithe, with a sense of purpose. It brought back memories of the night she'd spent curled up against him. Her imagination had run riot that night, wondering if there really was a set of hardened abs beneath all those layers of clothes. She'd love to find out.

"Whatever happened to that guy, Tony, was it?" She asked, breaking the silence.

He stopped and turned to face her, mouth pulled down in a scowl. "I never saw him again."

"Oh. Okay." Stella had been hoping for a bit more conversation. "Was he a friend from prison?"

Wyatt narrowed his black eyes slightly. "What makes you say that?" he asked a little too quickly.

"I'm not sure." It wasn't something she could put her

finger on, but there'd been an aura about him. And the fact Wyatt wasn't disagreeing with her, made her feel she was on the right track. But she let it go.

Joseph appeared, clattering down the wooden steps with his arms full of plates. "Oh, thank Christ the other barbecue is here. Quick, we need to get these ribs and steaks on the grill. Naomi told me she's bringing some guests down in a few minutes. We haven't even got half of the food on the table yet."

"I can help if you like," Wyatt offered. He followed Joseph back up the stairs, and Stella watched his retreating back. Was it always going to be this hard to talk to him? What did she see in the guy, anyway? He was taciturn, and way too earnest for her liking. He was plain hard work. But on the other hand, she'd seen a gentler side to him that night in the truck; knew there was a lot more going on in his mind than he let on. How did that saying go again? Still waters run deep? It was certainly true with Wyatt.

Her musings were cut short by the sound of voices. It must be Naomi and her guests already. Stella had no more time to think about Wyatt for the next hour, as more and more guests arrived and she was run off her feet, making sure the salads were topped up, and that there were plenty of hot ribs to eat. Wyatt helped, too, making sure everyone had a drink in their hands, and that the large fireplace was well stocked with wood.

Finally, Violet told her to grab something to eat. Everyone had been fed, and people were coming back for seconds, or thirds. Violet could handle it for the time being. Stella didn't need to be told twice; she was starving. Grabbing a plate, she loaded it up with roast pork and salad—there were no ribs left—and wandered through the crowd. There was Wyatt, standing on the fringes, with Cat, Levi, Emily, Tom, and Penny. She made her way over.

"Looks like we all had the same idea." Emily held up her plate of food. "Pity I didn't get to taste any of the ribs. Were they good?"

"I don't know," Stella laughed. "They were the first to go."

Emily turned to Tom, her gaze going serious. "I heard that Clayton is back in town. He must've been released from prison already."

Both Emily and Tom shot a compassionate glance in Cat's direction. Cat's face darkened, but she said nothing. The name rang a bell in Stella's memory. That's right, Penny had mentioned him just the other day. Clayton was the man who'd been falsely accused of lighting the fires—Stella had never met him because he'd left the ranch by the time she became the assistant cook—and he'd finally been released from jail after serving nearly six months for trying to abduct Cat. At the time, Stella wasn't really sure why Penny brought up the subject, the guy must be some sort of loser in her eyes. Maybe Penny felt sorry for him; she wasn't sure and hadn't pursued the subject.

"Sorry, Cat," Emily apologized. "But I thought you should know he'd been released."

"She's right," Tom added. "Better to hear it from a friend than find out by running into him on the street." He took a protective step closer to Emily.

Stella watched Penny out of the corner of her eye. Was it a trick of her imagination, or did Penny flinch at the mention of Clayton's name? If she had, she hid it well, because now her face was a picture of unruffled interest, nothing more, nothing less.

"Thanks for your concern," Cat said, adding a slight smile to soften her snarky words. "But I already knew that dodgy character was back in town, and I'm fine with it." Cat turned to Levi. "Speaking of dodgy characters, I forgot to ask you; did you hear anything about a kerfuffle at the Corner Café yesterday?" She changed the subject deftly, and perhaps Stella didn't blame her. The man had held a knife to her throat, and Stella didn't think she'd want to dwell on the topic either, if it were her.

This new topic sounded like some gossip from town. She noticed Wyatt had stopped eating, laying his half-eaten pork back on his plate.

"I just heard from Steph that something unusual went down," Cat continued.

"Yeah, I saw Jude this morning." Levi had to mean Jude Wilder, one of the sheriff's deputies. He and Levi were friends. "Two men were showing a photo around, seems as if they were looking for someone. Arlo didn't like the look of them and told them to get out of his café. Said they were bothering his customers and not to come back."

"I can imagine." Cat grinned, all of her ear piercings glinting in the weak winter sunlight.

Stella didn't know Arlo personally, but she'd heard from Cat and the other staff who frequented his café, that he was quite a character. An old hippie from way back, he wore colorful clothes and sported a long, gray beard.

"Were they cops, or something? Did they find who they were looking for?" Cat asked.

"Jude doesn't know. Supposedly, the guys disappeared after Arlo kicked them out." Levi lifted one eyebrow in disdain and Stella was hit by the similarity between the two brothers. Wyatt had the same jaunty lift to his eyebrows when he found something far-fetched. Levi had a dark, neatly trimmed beard, unlike Wyatt, who was clean-shaven. Stella liked the smooth look better.

"But like Jude said, he doesn't have time to go around following up on people who weren't even breaking the law." Levi continued.

Stella wasn't sure what the fuss was about. Surely, they got strangers coming through Stevensville all the time. What was the difference with these two? Wyatt paced backward and placed his plate on a nearby table. He'd hardly touched his food.

Stella was about to ask why he wasn't hungry, when Cat stepped in front of her, piercing her with that crystal-blue gaze. "We're taking a bunch of guests out on the snowmobiles. You should join us."

That sounded like fun. Stella had been on one or two hikes whenever she got a free hour or two, but Joseph rarely gave her time off.

"Wyatt is coming," Cat added.

"I am?" He raised one dark eyebrow, a surprised smile twisting his lips.

"You are," Cat instructed. "Dean wants us to take a large group out. We need all the minders we can get. Everyone's coming, even Levi and Penny." Cat tipped her chin toward Penny. Stella caught her friend's eye, and Penny nodded enthusiastically. It wasn't often they all got to go out and have fun together.

"I'm not sure what Joseph will—"

Cat waved her hand in the air. "That man has you tied to the kitchen too tight. It's time you got out and enjoyed yourself, for once. I'll go and ask Dean. Joseph won't dare to argue with him."

"I wouldn't be so sure about that," Big Tom laughed. "Joseph doesn't answer to anyone."

It *was* her job to stay in the kitchen, but Stella didn't say that. It'd be nice to get out on a snowmobile into the forest and enjoy the crisp winter's day. "It sounds like fun. But I'm not sure… I've never ridden a snowmobile before."

"You can ride behind Wyatt," Cat said, and turned away, but not before Stella caught the hint of a wicked gleam in her eye. Her stomach did a strange, slow somersault at the idea.

How was she supposed to sort out her confusing feelings about Wyatt, if her insides did a happy dance every time he was near? This wasn't helping at all. But it didn't sound like she could back out of it now.

Penny waggled her eyebrows in Stella's direction as they all put the plates on the table. She saw Wyatt frown at Penny's antics and cringed inside. Cat tapped Dean on the shoulder and had a quiet word in his ear. He gave his trademark grin and nodded enthusiastically. Then he climbed up on the nearest chair and conversation stopped, so people could listen.

"Okay, everyone who wants to go on this year's first snowmobile ride, go and grab some warm clothes. Then meet us up in the machinery shed in ten minutes. We've got thirty snowmobiles, which should be enough for everyone. Let's get this party started." Dean pumped his fist in the air and everyone cheered. Stella smiled. Dean really loved this. He loved his ranch, and he loved having guests here. She was glad to be part of this renewal process.

Stella let out a whoop of joy as cold air sliced past her cheeks. This was like flying, the fresh snow racing past below. The pure speed and the sound of the motor were exhilarating. Even more exhilarating was the fact that her arms were wrapped around Wyatt's waist.

"Having fun?" Wyatt laughed over his shoulder.

"Yes," Stella yelled. "This is great. I don't know why I haven't done it before."

A raft of snowmobiles spread out around them. Cat had placed them on the left fringe of the group and told them not to let anyone past and make sure no one got lost. Emily and Tom were in the lead on separate snowmobiles. Cat and Levi brought up the rear, rounding up the stragglers. And Dale and Penny were on the right flank, with all the guests corralled in the middle. Dean had wanted to come, but he'd given up his snowmobile to Mr. Darcy and his daughter, who'd turned up at the last second, wanting to join the ride. Dean was like that; he'd give the shirt off his back, if you needed it.

At first, she'd felt useless, sitting on the back of Wyatt's snowmobile, clinging to him like some kind of barnacle, their helmets bumping together every time he slowed down. But as she got used to the swishing, swaying movement, she relaxed a little, let go of her death-like grasp on Wyatt, learning to control her head, and finally started to enjoy the ride. It was a perfect day to be out in the forest. Snow still clung to the branches of the fir trees; a fresh layer had come down last night, covering the large drifts left behind by the blizzard. But this didn't compare to that morning they'd emerged from Wyatt's truck into a sparkling winter wonderland. That'd been truly magical. She was glad Dean had encouraged her to come today. She'd pretended to ignore Joseph's thin-lipped glance in her direction as she hurried to the machinery workshop.

A kid riding nearby—he couldn't have been more than thirteen or fourteen—swished closer. Then he ducked behind them and flew out on a tangent, doing a three-hundred-and-sixty degree turn in a large clearing, spraying glittering snow in a shroud behind him. Wyatt swung after him and Stella had to cling on tight. She leaned down low, mentally urging Wyatt on. It was almost like rounding up a stray cow on a cattle drive.

"Get back with the others," Wyatt said firmly. The boy grinned, and made his way back to the group, not seeming to care; he'd achieved what he wanted. Stella almost wished Wyatt would do the same thing. It must feel unbelievable to spin around and around like that, going so fast. They settled back into a uniform pace, keeping in line with the rest of the riders.

Out of the blue, Wyatt asked, "How's the fiancé doing?" His tone was even, but Stella wondered if the angle of his shoulders had changed.

At the mention of Armand, her mood deflated. She hadn't answered his texts. She was too angry. The texts had halted after that last one on New Year's Eve. How dare he threaten her? He didn't even have the decency to talk to her personally. Only cowards sent texts. She'd never break up with anyone over a text message.

"I don't think he's my fiancé anymore," she murmured quietly.

"What was that?" Wyatt called back over his shoulder.

"I'm not sure," she answered, leaning as close to his ear as her helmet would allow. "Things are...complicated between us."

That was the simple description. Her feelings towards Armand were mixed. They'd met at the Institute. She was in her first year, and he was in his last. Armand had helped her perfect her pastry techniques, spent hours in the kitchen with her after class, patiently talking her through a method until she had it perfected. He also helped her get her first apprenticeship in the Boulangerie Cartellier, a new bakery with an up-and-coming chef. She owed him. Something he didn't seem to want to let her forget. Armand was solid, dependable, responsible, all traits her mother revered. But he was also...dare she say it...boring. Wyatt, on the other hand, was anything but boring.

"You didn't look thrilled at the New Year's Eve party," he said, turning his head slightly so she could see his lips move. Their cheeks almost touched as she lay her chin on his shoulder.

"No, I wasn't. He wants me to go back to France."

"And what do you want?" His quiet words were almost

lost as the wind whipped past them. That was the crux of the matter, wasn't it?

CHAPTER FOUR

Wyatt concentrated on guiding the snowmobile around a large tree trunk. But he couldn't keep the subtle feeling of satisfaction from rising through his gut.

"I don't want to go back." They'd been Stella's exact words.

It sounded like Stella was having problems with her fiancé. That was a bad thing for her. She was clearly struggling with it emotionally; he should be more sympathetic. Then why did he suddenly feel lighter with the knowledge? Happy that she might yet be unattached.

When Cat had tricked him into staying today, he'd been mad as hell. It was supposed to be a quick trip out to the ranch to deliver the barbecue. Then she dropped the bombshell they were going to eat. And then the snowmobile ride. Wyatt had felt trapped. He didn't enjoy feeling trapped. It was a little sad that Cat and Levi thought they had to stoop to lying to get him to do things. But then, perhaps that might be as much his fault as it was theirs. He didn't make matters easy.

Cat had been dropping gentle nudges in Wyatt's direction ever since Christmas day. Obviously, he hadn't kept his infatuation with Stella as well hidden as he hoped. At first,

Cat had come home and conveyed some little anecdote of the funny things Stella had done or said that day. After Wyatt ignored those hints, she asked when he was going to start dating again. Telling him it was time to get back out there, dip a toe in the ocean, all those stupid, meaningless analogies. Soon enough, those questions turned into suggestions that maybe it was Stella he should ask out on a date.

When he'd had enough and finally responded by telling Cat that Stella had a boyfriend, she'd waved his protestations away with a snort.

"Everyone knows Stella has a fiancé back in France," she said, clicking her fingers. "But even I can tell that girl's not really in love with him. She barely talks about him. I think it's more of a security blanket, something for her to hold on to while she gets used to this new place."

"You don't know what's going on in her head," Wyatt had argued. "Maybe she just doesn't like to profess her feelings out loud."

Cat snorted again. "If she were truly in love with him, why is she not with him now?" Cat's question had resonated in Wyatt's mind for the rest of the day. Just because Cat and Levi were deliriously happy and hardly left each other's side, didn't mean that other people were the same. Lots of couples spent time apart, some even doing the long-distance thing successfully.

No amount of persuasion was going to change Wyatt's mind. After he found out about Stella's boyfriend, it was a perfect excuse to stay away. It was the kick in the pants he needed to decide she wasn't for him. And it was the main reason he wasn't going to come to the barbecue today. The less he saw of her, the better.

Until he was tricked into joining in.

There was another reason he didn't want to get involved with Stella. One that he would never confess to anybody. It'd taken a while to even admit it to himself. Stella seemed to have a special knack of being able to get him to open up when no one else could. That night spent in the truck, he'd talked to her more in those few hours than he'd possibly talked to anyone in his entire time in prison. She'd asked him at some stage why he wouldn't look at her properly, like he was afraid of her or something. She put it down to him being shy. He told her some bullshit story that he was like that because it was the only way he'd learned to keep himself safe in jail. They were like a pack of junkyard dogs in there, and the trick was to make yourself invisible. Not catch anyone's eye. Don't antagonize anyone.

But that wasn't why he wouldn't look directly at Stella. He certainly wasn't afraid of her. He *was* afraid that she would use that deep insight to see through the thin veneer of his humanity, down to his true self. And he really didn't think she'd like what she saw down there.

"This is so much fun. I'm glad Cat talked me into it." Stella was nestled into his back, moving with him as he swished through the snow. Her mouth was near his ear, wisps of her hair brushing against his cheek.

"You seem to spend a lot of time in the kitchen."

"It's my job," she quipped over his shoulder.

Her hands were clasped tightly across his stomach. Even through the layers of their bulky coats, he could feel her slender body and her breasts pressed up against his back. He enjoyed having her holding on to him. They were in their own intimate snowmobile bubble. Even though they were surrounded by all these other people and loud machines, it felt like just the two of them, alone together.

It also felt good to be part of this team. The staff at the Stargazer Ranch were a close-knit bunch, and they seemed to welcome him as one of them. He was relaxing around them a little more, now that he knew Cat and Levi hadn't told them about his stint in prison. Not that he didn't want people to know, he just wanted to tell them in his own good time. His story was a complicated one, and he hated to be misjudged.

It was also marvelous to be out amongst the forest again. It was one of the worst things about being cooped up behind bars. Wyatt had spent a lot of his teenage years—especially when he needed to get away from his drunken father—camping in the woodlands of the reservation. Surviving off the land, often for a week at a time. Now that he was living with Levi, he was once again taking advantage of the proximity of the mountains. He'd prowled around most of the hiking trails in the area over the past six months.

There was a blue flash in the trees above. "Look, a Steller's Jay." He pointed a finger, hoping Stella would see the pretty little bird in all its royal blue finery. It was an unusual sighting for winter, but not unheard of, especially if locals left out feeders, year-round. The bold, noisy bird was a pleasure to watch. "You have the same name."

"Wow," she breathed into his ear. "I didn't know there were such colorful birds here." It always amazed him that people knew so little about their natural surroundings. He began pointing out other things. The tracks of a raccoon in the soft snow. A string of icicles decorating the edge of a rocky overhang. The fluffy bounce of a white tail as a snowshoe hare disappeared down its burrow.

It seemed like only a few minutes had passed, but an hour later, the main lodge appeared over the last rise. It was late afternoon, the sun's rays touching the tips of the trees. Soon, the temperature would drop dramatically as night encroached. The ride was over, and Wyatt had to crush the ache of disappointment behind his ribcage, knowing Stella's arms would no longer be wrapped around his stomach.

"Wyatt, can you and Levi stay behind and help me get the snowmobiles all put away properly, please?" Cat called over the sound of people turning off their motors and chatting happily together.

"Sure thing," he replied, removing his helmet and hanging it over the handlebar.

"I should go... Joseph will need me," Stella whispered over his shoulder.

He grunted, but didn't reply. He could respect her work ethic, but it meant their time together was truly over.

Then, as if she had a change of heart, she said, "I guess a few more minutes won't hurt. I'll stay and help." She took off her helmet and shook out her messy bun, tendrils of hair falling around her face, replacing her protective headgear with her gray knit cap to keep the icy wind at bay.

Cat had a very specific way of setting up the snowmobiles, so they all fitted into the machinery workshop. Some guests were happy to drive theirs straight in, and so Cat directed them where to go.

Wyatt and Stella dismounted and stood off to the side, away from the mayhem of people lining up to get their snowmobiles in the door.

"How's she ever gonna sort this out?" Stella laughed, watching as two teenage boys tussled with each other, both wanting to be first in the door. Cheeks pink from the cold, and eyes bright from the exhilaration, Stella looked up into his face and he caught his breath. She was so damn beautiful. It was no wonder his mind went to porridge every time he looked at her. But while his mind went soft when he was around her, other parts of him went rock hard.

A few of the guests had left their snowmobiles parked to the side, unable or unwilling to put them away. Wyatt walked over to the first one and pushed the start button, so it was idling, then began to direct it inside.

"I'll help," Stella said.

"They're heavy and awkward to move," he warned.

"I'm strong." She held up one arm and flexed her bicep, and he had to laugh.

"Right, well, start them up and use the throttle gently to help you shift them." He liked that she wanted to be involved. She was eager to try everything, do everything. They joined the back of the line, but it moved quickly, and it didn't take long to get inside.

He showed her how to swing the snowmobile around and back it into the slot next to his. She struggled to turn hers, but held up her hand to ward him off when he made to come and help her, determined to do this by herself. He stood back and watched, liking the little grunting noises she made as she dug her heels into the dirt and maneuvered the heavy machine.

With a satisfied smile, she looked up when she finally got it parked just right and turned it off. His heart did a strange double-thump in his chest. They went out and got another snowmobile each to bring in. Cat and Levi were at the back of the workshop when they brought the next two in, rearranging some snowmobiles to get them exactly to Cat's liking. Everyone else had left. He swung his machine into place and then watched as Stella navigated this one with more ease.

But as she backed it in next to his, she let out a little cry of pain. "*Zut*," she muttered.

His head whipped around. "What's the matter?"

"Nothing," she said, looking at him with a guilty tilt to her mouth.

But it wasn't nothing, she was nursing her left hand.

"What did you do?" He was already reaching for her, tugging off her glove.

"I jammed my little finger between the two handlebars. It's nothing, really." But she didn't pull back, instead, letting him turn her hand over so he could inspect the damage to her bare finger. Removing his gloves, he could feel her hands were icy, despite the protection of her own gloves.

He winced as he saw a large blood blister already forming on the side of her finger. That would've hurt. Gently probing, he moved the joints around to make sure nothing was broken. She winced, but didn't pull away. At least she wasn't screaming, which was a good sign nothing was damaged.

To keep her mind off what he was doing, he asked her quietly, "What was that word you said just then? Was it some kind of French swear word?"

"What? You mean *zut*?" She giggled as she said the word, and he nodded. "It means…how would you say it?" She tilted head up as if trying to find the right word. "Perhaps something like shucks."

"Ah, I thought you're going to teach me a really cool new French swear word. I mean, everyone's heard *merde*, but I'd never heard of that one before."

He put her chilly hand between his two, much warmer ones, and held them up to his mouth, blowing warm air over her frozen fingers. His lips rested gently against the side of her hand as he stared down into her leaf-green eyes. It was only then he realized how close they were standing. Face still flushed a tantalizing pink from the cold, she sucked in her bottom lip as she watched what he was doing. Tendrils of mahogany hair coiled out from beneath her knit cap. He brushed one of them aside, feeling the softness of her cheek. His gaze found her lips, and despite himself, he couldn't look away, fascinated by the way her mouth curled up. Rose-red and glistening as her tongue darted out and then back in again. The memory of kissing those lips, of the tiny sound she made when she opened to invite him in, came back to light a fire deep in his gut.

He leaned in to taste her, unable to stop himself. She stood on tiptoe, meeting him halfway. Injury forgotten, he dropped her hand so he could pull her in tighter.

She made that slight sound, a cross between a whimper and a groan as he claimed her lips and his guts contracted. That sound drove all the way to his core, lighting his blood on fire and making him want to find the nearest bed and throw her onto it.

She opened her mouth, tempting him to go deeper. His hand went around her slim waist, nestling in the small of her back, bringing her closer. He closed his eyes and let the moment overtake him. She was sweet like strawberries and cream. But there was also something darker, a hunger he hadn't felt during their first kiss.

A noise from nearby had him suddenly remembering where they were. Wyatt quickly glanced up. Cat and Levi were both still at the rear of the work-shed, arguing about the right way to park the snowmobiles. Their backs were turned, their heads together in conversation. Wyatt wondered if they'd seen anything. Cat would be sure to let him know if she had soon enough, anyway.

Stella looked up and drew in a shaky breath. "Oh, wow. I couldn't..." She didn't finish her sentence, merely stared up at him, a mixture of yearning and confusion in her eyes.

Before their moment could be completely stolen away, Wyatt said the first thing that came to him. "I'd like to make you dinner one night."

What had he just said? He was asking Stella on a date. And wouldn't that make Cat happy? But he was prepared to put up with her smug smile, if only Stella would say yes. It was against his better wisdom. And who knew where it would lead? All he truly recognized was that he needed to see her again. Back when they'd been snowbound in the truck together, she'd been fascinated by the fact he loved to cook and that he worked at CJ's Burger joint. He'd promised that he'd cook for her one day. And this might be his chance.

"Really?" A slow smile spread across her gorgeous face.

Was that a yes or no? Wyatt held his breath.

She cocked her head to the side. "I'd like to taste your cooking."

He thought that might be a yes. "What about tomorrow night?"

Her face crumpled into a frown. "I'm scheduled on all week for dinner service. It's opening week, so many guests will be checking in."

His mind raced. "What time do you normally finish?"

Stella pursed her lips. "Most of the guests have finished by half-past eight. I could ask Violet to cover for me after that."

"That's perfect." Wyatt could work around that. It wasn't ideal, he'd rather have an early dinner and show her the sunset, but he could still make this work. "I'll come and pick you up. We'll make it a quick dinner, I promise." He knew she'd need to be back to start her shift early the next morning.

"Okay...that would be lovely." She only hesitated for a split second before her smile returned, but it was enough to make Wyatt wonder. Had she been thinking about the fiancé? He tried to put that out of his mind. It'd definitely be a topic of conversation on their date—if that's what it was. They needed to clear the air once and for all, if this was to go any further. He wasn't the type of man to date another guy's chick. That wasn't his style. But this was one dinner, and no more. No expectations, no promises. A bit of fun, for once.

"I'll walk you down to the lodge," he said, taking her hand and helping her replace her glove.

He turned his head toward the other couple. "See you down at the truck." Cat waved vaguely in his direction and he turned back to Stella. "You should put some ice on your finger. It'll help stop any further swelling."

"Thank you, I'll do that." She looked at him and then swung her gaze away. But not before he saw all the questions in her eyes. They were the same questions echoing around his head. They walked in companionable silence, down the small hill and up to the rear of the lodge. There were still signs left over from all the construction that'd taken place. It would take a while for the new sections to weather in, so they looked like the rest of the buildings. But Dean, with the contractor's help, had done an outstanding job; if you didn't know any better, you almost wouldn't see where the new met the old.

"How's the new kitchen turning out?" he asked, as they stopped by the back door.

"It's much better than the old one. Joseph helped the designer get it perfect. I love the huge, new gas stove, we can cook up to eight dishes at a time." He'd clearly asked the right question, as the words gushed out of Stella's mouth. He liked to watch her animated face, the way she talked with her hands, as well as her eyes. "Although, I miss the beautiful old table we used to sit around having our meals. I think it might've belonged to Dean's grandfather. It had a history, you know? Dean had another one especially built, and it suits the kitchen better, perhaps. But…"

Wyatt had never seen the old table, he arrived back in town around the same time as Cyrus had attacked the lodge. He could see what Stella was trying to say, however. The French had a long history. It seemed she liked things that held a certain antiquity.

"But it doesn't have the same sentimental value," he finished for her.

"That's exactly it." Her beaming smile told him he'd hit the nail on head.

"Well, I'd better get to the truck. I've got a shift tonight at CJ's." He hoped Cat would be down soon to drive him into town. If not, she could explain to Bryce why he was late for work.

"Thank you for the snowmobile ride, Wyatt."

"No problems. I'll see you tomorrow night."

"Yes, tomorrow," she agreed.

He turned to go, but she grabbed his hand and pulled him in, kissing him gently on both cheeks in the French way.

"*Au revoir*, Wyatt."

Oh, sweet Jesus, that accent was going to drive him crazy with desire.

Five minutes later, as Cat drove—with an annoyingly smug smile on her face—Wyatt sat staring out the side window. The conversation at the barbecue played on his mind. Tony had never shown up yesterday to collect his package. Which'd left Wyatt unsettled. Tony was unreliable and unpredictable, and so Wyatt had shrugged it off. But this news of two strangers in town made the hairs on the back of his neck stand up. Could they be connected? Wyatt would love to have seen the photo those two were showing around. Who were they looking for? Why hadn't Tony shown up? He'd taken the extreme chance of stealing a car to come out and demand his package back, which demonstrated desperation. But then hadn't come to collect it when he said he would. It was more than a little odd. Had Tony got wind of something going down?

Wyatt had Tony's backpack stashed in his bedroom, unsure whether to return it to its hiding place or wait until Tony showed up.

Perhaps it was time to take a look at whatever was in that bag.

CHAPTER FIVE

Stella swiped a hand across her sweaty brow. *Zut*. It was already twenty minutes past eight. Wyatt would be here soon. She still had to stack all the dishes into the dishwasher, and then she had to go and get changed. She couldn't go out like this, with splotches of pasta sauce on her T-shirt, and her face red with perspiration from rushing around the heated kitchen.

At least the dinner service was over. When people visited the country, they seemed to become hungry earlier. In France, they rarely ate until nine or ten o'clock, especially during summer. But here, in the dead of winter, people were getting ready for their bed by then.

Roxanne, one of the waitresses, came in with a handful of plates and dumped them on the counter. "Don't you have to get fixed up for your big date?"

What? Did everybody know she was going to dinner with Wyatt? How had they found out? Stella glanced sideways, and it all became crystal clear. Violet was busily pretending to ignore them, as she plated up the last two pieces of apple pie.

"Here you go," she said to Roxanne. "Service up."

"Enjoy your date," Roxanne sang loudly as she went through the door and into the restaurant.

"Violet," Stella growled. "I asked you to keep it a secret. I don't need everybody knowing my business." Especially not when they still thought she had a fiancé. What must they think of her?

"I only told Roxanne," Violet said, not quite meeting Stella's eye.

There was a beat of silence while Stella stared at her.

"And maybe Janine. But that's all, I swear."

Stella let out an agitated breath. Janine was the other waitress. Between the two of them, they'd probably told the whole ranch by now.

"But Roxy is right, you need to go, or you'll be late." Violet made shooing motions with her hands. "I've got this; go on, off you go. Quick, before Joseph comes back and finds something else for you to do." They both glanced in unison at the door to the restaurant. Joseph was currently out on the floor, doing his nightly rounds. He liked to talk to the guests and was at his obsequious best, charming them all.

How could Stella stay mad at Violet? After all, she was doing her a big favor by staying late to finish up for her. And she was right; if she went now, she could make good her escape.

"Thank you, Violet." She whipped off her apron and dunked it in the wash basket. Then, she grabbed her coat from the hook in the hall, and was still pulling it on as she went out the back door. How was she ever going to get used to this cold weather? It took her breath away as she jogged the short distance between the lodge and the single-staff quarters. It was freezing out here, after the heat of the kitchen. She hoped Wyatt had somewhere warm and private in mind for dinner.

A shiver of anticipation went through her.

Having dinner with Wyatt—she didn't want to call it a date, because she wasn't sure that's what it was, yet—was still hard to believe.

Harder to accept was how she'd broken up with Armand last night. She'd called him on her cell. Lyon was eight hours ahead of Montana, so it was late when she spoke to him. The time difference was one more thing making communication difficult.

At least she had the guts to tell him over the phone. Not like him, sending cowardly texts, making half-hearted threats and nasty jibes. His final text, where he'd threatened to call off the engagement if she didn't come home, had been the last straw.

The door to the staff quarters loomed, and she stomped the snow from her sneakers before turning the handle to go inside.

Five minutes. That's all the time she had to get ready. She'd already planned what she was going to wear tonight, and it was laid out on her single bed, in the room she shared with Penny. Jeans and a pink, cashmere sweater. It was warm and practical, but she also knew the color set off her green eyes.

She went into the bathroom, splashed water on her face, brushed her hair, and pulled it into the loose top knot she always wore. Back in the bedroom she changed and then quickly applied some foundation to cover the worst of the scar on her forehead and then a touch of light-pink lip gloss.

Armand had not been happy. He'd shouted, something he seldom ever did. Even calling her a *putain*, a whore. Which was completely out of line and uncharacteristic. Armand rarely stooped to that sort of language. She'd tried to remain cool and logical, the opposite to his heat and anger.

It hurt that she'd hurt him. He didn't deserve it. Armand had only ever been good to her. He couldn't help the way he was. He couldn't help it if she'd outgrown him. But when she said that old cliche line, *it's not you, it's me*, he'd hung up in disgust. Perhaps when he cooled down, he might admit there were some grains of truth in what she'd said. They weren't suited. All he wanted was to settle down, have a family, and grow his patisserie into a franchise. Which were all wonderful goals. But none of them made her heart beat faster.

She smudged her lip gloss and cursed. Grabbing a tissue, she wiped it off and started again.

Armand had asked her if there was someone else. She denied it. Because he was only looking for another excuse for her change of heart. He couldn't bear to think he was the problem. Wyatt wasn't the reason she was breaking up with Armand. If she was truthful, she might admit he was the catalyst, but he wasn't the reason. Stella had moved to Montana in a bid to widen the gap between her and Armand. She hadn't been happy with him, even back in France. This'd been coming for a long time.

What would Wyatt think when she told him? If she told him. This was all too new, and...bewildering. She wasn't sure if there was anything there with Wyatt. And even if there was, he had a past that scared her a little. Even Wyatt admitted his time in jail had changed him. But Stella liked to believe everyone deserved another chance. Everyone had some good in them. You had to dig deeper to find it in some people, that was all.

The sound of the front door opening drifted down the hallway to her bedroom, interrupting her thoughts. She glanced at her cell phone. It was eight-forty.

Zut. She was late. Her bulky, Stargazer coat lay on her bed, but she peered into her closet, trying to decide which jacket would be better tonight. She'd brought a long, black jacket with her from France, it was from Musier, and she hadn't had a chance to wear it yet. Remembering just how cold it was out there, Stella finally erred on the side of practicality, and picked up the Stargazer coat. All the staff were issued with one; it had the Stargazer Ranch logo on the back. When she wore it, it made her feel like she was part of the team, even if she hardly ever went outside.

She bounced down the hall and rounded into the shared lounge area. There was Wyatt, sitting on the couch, waiting for her. He was wearing the same black, sheepskin jacket and black jeans he'd had on yesterday; it seemed to be his signature outfit. Although, tonight, he also had a gray hoodie on underneath the jacket. He looked outdoorsy and mysterious, and sexy as hell.

A slow smile curved his lips upward as he took her in. "You look nice." His gaze tumbled from top of her head to the tip of her toes. His expression sent a shiver down her spine. There was dark hunger in his eyes. She liked that he appreciated the view.

"Where are we going tonight?" She was suddenly flustered, asking the first thing that came to mind.

"I'm taking you back to my place."

That was interesting. She hid her surprise with a bright grin. "Oh, great."

"I hope you don't mind?" he said, as if catching her slight hesitation. "I've got a picnic planned."

Wow, he was full of surprises. She held up her Stargazer coat. "Lucky I've brought this then."

"And your hat and gloves, too?"

She patted one of her coat pockets. "I always keep them in here. Shall we go?" She waited while he stood and then preceded him out the door. One thing was for sure, Wyatt was unpredictable. That was one of the reasons she was drawn to him. She would never have guessed in her wildest dreams their dinner would include a picnic, at night, in the middle of winter. Life wasn't dull with Wyatt around. And she was invariably up for something new.

There was silence in the cab for the first few minutes of the drive. But Stella was getting used to Wyatt's taciturn ways, and she began to chat about her workday, telling him how Joseph had yelled at her for spilling the crackers all over the floor. Her mother used to say that she would natter on about nonsense, but Stella didn't mind. It was true; she liked to fill a silence. Perhaps that showed a lack of self-confidence, who knew? But Wyatt didn't seem to mind. He even gave her an encouraging smile, now and then. And it was better for her to chatter away, rather than let thoughts of how she and Wyatt had lain together on this very bench seat in his truck all night. Even though nothing had happened between them, it still bought heat to her cheeks to remember the intimacy of being curled up together, trying to stay warm.

When they pulled into his driveway, he told her to stay where she was. Then he ran around and tugged the door open with a chivalrous twist of his wrist. He was so sweet.

She followed Wyatt up the wooden porch steps and through the front door. As Wyatt closed the door behind them, she heard a scrabbling sound. Something gray and fury came hurtling down the hall toward them. She recoiled into Wyatt's chest.

"What is that?" she squeaked.

"Sorry, I forgot to warn you about Rekker. He's Levi's tame raccoon." Wyatt moved between her and the animal, trying to shoo him away.

"No, don't, he's cute. Can I pet him?" Stella got down on her knees and cautiously reached out a hand.

"You can try," Wyatt said with a cynical lift to his eyebrow. "Cat can pet him, but not me. Maybe he prefers women."

The raccoon came forward and stood up on his hind legs to sniff her outstretched hand. His whiskers tickled her fingers, and she giggled. Then she gently ran her palm over his ears and down his silky fur. He seemed to like it, as he raised his paws again, as if begging for more.

"Little traitor," Wyatt muttered.

Levi appeared through a door at the end of the hallway, Cat half a step behind him, and Stella stood. Even though she knew Wyatt lived with his brother and Cat, she hadn't expected them to be here. Which was probably a little naïve of her.

"Oh, hi," she said, not sure if she should be embarrassed that they were here, witnessing her and Wyatt's first date. But was it even the date? She didn't know.

"Hey, Stella, good to see you," Levi called down the hallway. "I've got the patties in the oven, all ready to go, just like you said." His gaze shifted to Wyatt, and there was a question mark in the lift of his eyebrow.

"Thanks, bro." Wyatt grabbed her hand and towed her up the hall behind him. To Stella he said, "I've got a couple of quick things to do in the kitchen, then our picnic will be ready."

She wasn't sure if she was looking forward to a picnic in the cold and dark. But as they rounded through the kitchen door, she could see Wyatt had gone to a lot of trouble. There was a large backpack on the table, half-filled with containers of food, and the makings of a meal still scattered on the countertops.

She loved poking around in other folks' kitchens. Perhaps it was because food was so important in her life. If she'd been alone, she may well have opened cupboards to see how they kept their kitchen provisioned. For her, it was like peering into people's souls; a kitchen could tell you a lot about a person. But this was Levi and Cat's kitchen, not Wyatt's, so she probably wouldn't learn much about him, anyway.

Wyatt bustled between the oven and the countertop.

"You're in for a treat tonight," Cat said, leaning against the door frame, her blonde hair spiked and blue eyes sparkling. She seemed to be enjoying this. "Wyatt spent hours in the kitchen this afternoon creating a special burger just for you."

"Really?" Stella tried to peer around Wyatt's back, to see what he was doing with the patties he'd taken out of the oven.

"Cat, you're supposed to let Wyatt tell her that," Levi scolded. He went over and slipped his arm around her waist, taking the sting out of his words.

Cat merely shrugged. What everyone else thought never bothered her.

Stella heard the crumple of paper, and then Wyatt turned with two wrapped burgers in his hands. They looked exactly like they might've come straight from a fast-food joint, and she laughed as she remembered she'd said she wanted to taste one of Wyatt's burgers. If they'd been in France, she would have expected candlelit tables, soft music, and an expensive restaurant. But this was Wyatt, always doing something unexpected.

"I've got some heat pads in here, to keep the food warm," Wyatt said, tucking the burgers into the top of the backpack. "Are you ready to go?"

Stella nodded, even though she had no idea where they were going, or how they were going to get there.

"It's a five-minute walk down to the river," he told her. "I've got a flashlight for both of us."

Stella sucked in a deep breath. "It sounds like an adventure."

"There's a place I want to show you. I hope you enjoy it."

As she pulled her knit cap and gloves out of her pocket, Wyatt handed her a thick, hand-knitted, woolen scarf. "I thought you might need this."

"Thank you." She took the proffered scarf and wrapped it around her neck. It was so sweet, him thinking of her. "Can I carry anything?"

"There's a Thermos of hot chocolate over there." Wyatt pointed to the countertop. "Can you manage that?"

"Of course I can."

As she picked it up, Wyatt gave her one of his rare smiles and her heart jolted in her chest. Suddenly, she didn't care that she was about to go out into the freezing wilderness and picnic in the dark. All she cared about was the fact she was going to be with Wyatt.

As they were about to walk out the back door, Levi said abruptly, "Oh, I nearly forgot. Your buddy came looking for you again. The same guy who was at the New Year's Eve party."

Wyatt stopped, his hand on the door handle. He turned around slowly, his face thunderous.

"What did he want?"

CHAPTER SIX

Wyatt frowned. Tony had been here, at the house, looking for him? That slimy weasel. Why hadn't he turned up when he said he was going to? Wyatt had been so tempted to take a look at the bulky package, wrapped in brown paper, in Tony's backpack. But time and circumstance had gotten in the way, and somehow he'd never had a chance. Now he wished he had. Waiting for Levi's answer, he tried not to grind his teeth. Stella glanced up at him, a question in the purse of her lips.

"He didn't say what he wanted, and I don't know if he's coming back." Levi let go of Cat's waist and stood up straighter.

"How did he seem?" Wyatt persisted.

"What do you mean?" Levi leaned both hands on the table and glared at Wyatt, while Cat watched the exchange with interest.

"I dunno. Was he happy, sad, in a hurry?" Wyatt really wanted to ask if he looked agitated or scared, but he didn't want to worry Levi.

"It was hard to tell. He's not my friend, after all." Levi stared at him, and the tension in the room ramped up. He must've sensed there was something else going on.

"Never mind," Wyatt turned away, reaching for the door handle again.

"Look, bro, he didn't say much. He mentioned that he'd been around to see you at work, and you weren't there, so he dropped by here, just in case."

Jesus. He didn't need Tony meddling in his affairs. And he didn't want Tony going around to his place of work asking questions, either. It was bad enough he came round to his house, making Levi and Cat suspicious. Stella was still looking at him, eyes wide. So, he put Tony and all that he entailed to the back of his mind. He was going on a picnic with Stella; that was all that mattered right now.

"It's all good, I'll catch up with him another day. Come on Stella, let's go, before our food gets cold."

She followed him silently out the door, and he tried to shake off the unease Levi's words left behind. He flicked on his flashlight, and Stella did the same behind him. He liked the fact she didn't ask questions—because she must have plenty—but she was keeping them to herself. There was a hidden gate cut into the high, wooden fence running along the rear of Levi's house. Lifting the latch, he let them both through, and closed it again. A faint trail ran downhill, across a patch of cleared land, and disappeared into the dense undergrowth. Levi and Cat had made a private walkway down to the river. It'd become his favorite place; he went there nearly every day.

Was he being a complete idiot for taking Stella down there? He'd been so happy, when she agreed to come to dinner with him, it was the first spot that'd popped into his mind. He wanted to share it with her. This was what he loved, and this was who he was. He felt safer outdoors in the wilderness. No one to tell him what to do, just the animals and the wind sighing through the trees to keep him company. What if she hated it? Didn't like the cold or the dark, or both? She was a city girl, and probably used to the finer things in life.

He glanced quickly behind, to make sure Stella was following him. She'd done extremely well enduring their night spent caught in the blizzard. After her initial shock and horror at their predicament, she'd been accepting, almost embracing the experience as some kind of new adventure.

"Watch out, the trail gets steep here." He stopped and offered her his hand to help her down the rocky slope. She took it, and he felt the buzz of connection flow up his arm. "Not far now," he promised.

"I can hear the river," she replied. "Doesn't it ice over in the winter?"

He kept hold of her hand, even after the trail flattened out. "Around the edges it does, but it's too deep and fast-flowing in the middle to freeze all the way over. You'll see what I mean in a minute."

The sound of rushing water got louder, and all of a sudden, the oppressive, dark forest opened to reveal the night sky. The Bitterroot River was about three-hundred feet wide here. In some places it was shallow, gurgling over rounded rocks and through fast-flowing rapids, and in other places it was deep and dangerous. Like this spot he'd brought her to tonight. He could sit by the river for hours, letting it wash away his cares and his petty worries.

"There's a little beach over here." He pointed his flashlight to the left. The beam of light picked out the pile of sticks and brush, surrounded by a ring of rocks he'd laid earlier this afternoon, waiting to be lit.

He stopped at the boundary of the small, pebble beach, placing his backpack on the ground. "Wait here a second."

Dropping to his knees, he pulled out a lighter and set fire to the dry tinder. Almost immediately, flames licked skywards. He made sure he'd laid the fire just right, so it'd catch quickly. It was something he was good at, after all his time spent alone in the forests around his reservation. Then he unzipped the backpack and drew out the thick blanket he'd packed on top. The food was still warm, and he quickly arranged it all on the blanket.

"Come and sit down." He patted the spot next to him.

Stella had her head tipped back, staring at the stars, and when she looked down at him, he could see them reflected in her eyes. She crossed her legs and settled in beside him, and he pulled out another blanket from the bottom of his backpack, wrapping it around her shoulders.

"Oh, thank you. This is much nicer than I was expecting. You've thought of everything."

"Did you think I was going to make you freeze in the dark?"

He caught the flash of her white teeth in the dimness as she smiled. She was sitting so close, if he leaned toward her slightly, their shoulders would touch.

"The truth?" She gave a soft giggle. "I really didn't know what to expect. But this is lovely." They locked gazes for a second. "What about you? Do you have a blanket?"

"I've got another one in my bag. But I'm tough; I don't feel the cold." He gave her a cheeky grin. After so much time spent outdoors, it was true. He'd much rather feel the sting of an icy wind on his cheeks and know he was alive, than be cooped up inside. Which was one of the many reasons being locked up for two years in prison had just about killed him.

"You must be starving," he said, handing her one of the packages he'd wrapped up in the kitchen. It was late, and he was hungry; his stomach had been rumbling for more than an hour now. But it was worth the wait, so he could eat with Stella.

"What in it?" She asked, unwrapping the paper and lifting the burger to her nose, inhaling deeply.

"It's something special I concocted for you. I hope you like blue cheese," he asked, suddenly worried.

She laughed. "I'm French, remember? Of course I do." She took a large bite. "Mmm, what is that sauce?"

"It's a beetroot relish I made the other day. There's also grilled peppers, and baked eggplant."

"It's delicious," she mumbled through a mouthful. "When you said you liked to experiment with food, I wasn't sure what you meant, but this is superb."

"Thank you." It was nice to hear praise for his food, especially from her.

"Do you make this at your burger joint?"

"No." Wyatt gave a cynical grunt. "Bryce isn't the most imaginative cook. To him, a burger is a burger. He'd think I'd gone mad, if I suggested adding blue cheese." Wyatt grimaced at the idea. He liked Bryce, respected him for giving him a chance. Even though Wyatt was acquitted and found innocent, people still judged him. They couldn't see past the fact he was an ex-con. At least Bryce had the decency to study Wyatt's credentials.

Bryce had belonged to a biker gang, back in his youth. And he still had the tattoos to prove it. He was gruff and a little surly, but always kept his beard neatly trimmed, and his kitchen sparkling clean. Wyatt didn't mind if Bryce wasn't innovative. He ran a strict kitchen, cooked traditional burgers that the locals loved, and made a satisfactory living. He was a good man, and in some ways, he was a man to look up to. If Wyatt could have a life similar to Bryce's, then perhaps he could be happy, or at the very least content.

"This is amazing. I'm sure Bryce would change his mind once he tasted it." Stella held the burger up and scrutinized it, turning it from side to side. "You could serve this in any gourmet restaurant. It's perfect. The meat patty is incredible. What do you put in it to make it taste so good? And look at the way the cheese melts down the outside."

He took a bite of his own burger and watched her face by the light of the fire. It came alive when she talked. The French were more animated than Americans, and he loved to watch her face, read the expressions that crossed her features as she spoke. Warm breath came out in a drift of steam, and his eyes were drawn to her mouth. He no longer heard her words, merely concentrated on the movement of her mouth, the way her lips curved upward.

She stopped talking, pursed her lips and focused her gaze on him.

Uh-oh, she must've asked him a question, and he missed it. "Sorry, what?"

A sexy smile passed over her face, almost as if she knew what he'd been up to. "I asked how you found this place. I would never have thought to come here, not in a million years."

He shrugged. "I spent most of my teenage years hiking and camping out in the woods. It's easy for me to be outside. These places are everywhere, if you stop and look. It's one of the reasons I never moved far away from these mountains."

"Your life has been so different to mine," she admitted. "I grew up in the city streets. My mother never took me camping, she hates the outdoors." Stella stated it like a fact, but Wyatt also heard a note of regret in her voice.

He already knew a little about her childhood, from their time together during the blizzard. Knew she had no brothers or sisters, and no father in the picture, either. Understood that her relationship with her mother was complicated. But most mother-daughter relationships were complicated, weren't they?

"But I wouldn't change my life for the world, because I love being a pastry chef, and I love working at Stargazer. And I love being here with you."

He wasn't sure how to respond. It was true; they were two

different people, and maybe this dinner had been a mistake. Perhaps they'd decide they really were completely unsuitable. There was the fiancé, for one thing. Was he truly out of the picture? Or was there a chance it was merely a hitch in their relationship? And if he was still in the picture, where could they possibly go from here? But there was something about Stella that called to him. He didn't know what it was, and he couldn't explain it. All he knew was that she made him feel better when she was around. More as if he belonged, and less like he was living his life on the fringes of society.

Stella finished the burger and wiped her mouth with the crumpled paper.

He took the paper from her fingers and said, "I've got warm, homemade brownies, and hot chocolate in that Thermos you carried down. Would you like some?"

Stella groaned. "My stomach is about to pop, but that sounds so good, I have to try some."

He unwrapped the brownies. The heat pad inside the backpack had kept them warm and gooey. This was a recipe he'd perfected, using Levi and Cat as guinea pigs. Cat had complained she was putting on weight since he'd moved in, but she never refused the offer of a brownie. Wyatt poured the milky chocolate into two tin mugs.

Stella got to her feet, and pulled the blanket tighter around her shoulders. Then she picked up her brownie in one hand and a mug of hot chocolate in the other and wandered toward the edge of the river. Surprised, he grabbed his own mug and sweet treat and followed her.

"I need to stand up, to shake all that food down," she laughed.

"Are you warm enough?"

"I'm perfect, thank you." She tilted her head to look up at him. Now they were away from the fire, there was only starlight to light her features. Her soft, gray, knit cap sat low on her forehead, covering her ears and framing the oval of her face. And the scarf he'd lent to her was tucked up tight under her chin, making her look soft and inviting. She took a step toward him. "Actually, I've never felt warmer."

He wanted to kiss her. The night they'd spent together a little over a week ago, trapped in his truck, had brought them closer. He'd heard that feelings forged in adversity were often much stronger; connections formed quicker than normal that way. Whatever it was, he felt as if he knew Stella, like they'd been familiar for many months, not merely a few days.

"There's something I need to tell you," she said quietly, but he was hardly listening. Her presence was affecting his capacity to do anything normal.

They were alone together, standing beneath the night sky, with nothing and no one to interrupt them. His blood fired hot through his veins as he stepped toward her, brownie falling forgotten from his fingers. This would be different to when he kissed her under the mistletoe. He didn't want to hear whatever it was she needed to tell him. He wanted to get lost in this moment.

"Can I kiss you, first?" His lips hovered above hers.

Her gaze sought his, still filled with starlight. "Please." Her single word was a breath of air.

He required no more encouragement. His mouth found hers.

The hot chocolate burned his fingers as it lapped over the edge of his mug. Dropping the tin mug with a clang on the pebbles, he used his now-free hand to gather her up closer. She jumped at the sound, but then did the same with her mug, burying her hand into the neck of his coat, standing on tiptoe to reach his mouth.

He tasted the sweet chocolate on her tongue, licked it from her lips. He suddenly wished they were no longer outside.

He wanted to rip the bulky overcoat off her slim frame, run his hands over her hips, feel her rounded butt through the fabric of her jeans. It was all he could do to stop his jaw from dropping open when she'd walked into the room earlier in those skin-tight blue jeans, and that cute pink sweater. She'd looked amazing.

Stella drew in small, breathless gasps, but she didn't break their kiss, pulling his mouth down onto her lips so he was left with no uncertainty as to how much she wanted this.

A faint sound reached his ears. Wyatt ignored it, letting the noise of the rushing water beside them drown it out. But soon, the sound got louder and morphed into a voice, calling his name. Stella seemed not to have heard, still lost in their passion.

"Wyatt."

Shit. It was Levi.

"Wyatt, I know you're there, I can see your fire. Answer me."

Stella flinched and pulled away, finally hearing Levi. He had to hand it to his brother, at least he hadn't come barreling onto the little beach, with no regard to what they might be up to. Instead, he'd stopped just outside the glow from the fire, where the grass first met the rocks. Wyatt sighed and lifted his head. Even out here in the middle of nowhere, he couldn't kiss Stella without being disturbed.

"What do you want?" He asked flatly, but there was an edge to his question that would make Levi understand he was not amused at being interrupted.

"Your friend, Tony just turned up again."

"Tell him to go away." Wyatt refused to relinquish his hold on Stella, still hoping that Levi would go away and leave them alone, and they could get back to what they'd been doing. She squirmed and looked up into his face, then pushed gently on his chest. Shit, the spell was broken. He let go of her, ready to round on his brother and tell him exactly what he thought of him.

"You need to come and talk to him. Now, Wyatt. Something's happened. Something terrible."

Wyatt froze. What was he talking about?

CHAPTER SEVEN

Stella couldn't believe what she was hearing. She scrubbed a hand across her eyes, and blinked. They were all sitting around the kitchen table. Cat and Levi on one side, her and Wyatt opposite, with Tony on the end, agitated and tapping his toe. Levi had his cell phone up to his ear, talking quietly, but urgently, into it.

Part of Stella remained caught in the moment of kissing Wyatt. Her lips were still warm and wanting more, and her brain was still firing on overload, her senses full of him. The smell of him. The feel of him. The way he surrounded her. But then Levi's call had snapped her out of her dreamlike state, and she was trying to get her intellect to fire on all four cylinders again. Even the fact that they'd hurriedly cleaned up the campsite and put out the campfire, then walked up the trail behind Levi, almost at a jog, had her a little disoriented.

"Say that again." Wyatt scrubbed a hand through his hair. She could tell by the complete bewilderment on his face, he was having a hard time trusting what Tony had just told them.

"Bryce is dead, dude."

Wyatt shook his head, confusion and anger clouding his eyes, as if Tony were speaking a foreign language.

Levi put his cell down on the kitchen table. Both Levi and Wyatt had beautiful bronze skin; Stella loved the color, it reminded her of caramel fudge candy. But right now, Levi's face was as pale as the white wall behind him.

"That was Jude, he's at the scene. He wouldn't give me any details, of course, but he confirmed Tony's story. Bryce is dead."

Stella put a hand to her mouth to cover her gasp. She'd never met the man, but this was terrible. Her gaze darted to Wyatt. What must he be thinking? What must he be feeling? His face was closed, eyes narrowed and focused on the tabletop, as if he'd withdrawn into himself.

"I told ya," Tony said. "But you wouldn't believe me. He was gunned down, I'm telling ya."

Levi backed him up by saying, "Jude wouldn't corroborate how he was killed. But by the sound of his voice, it was pretty serious." He fixed his gaze on his older brother, and Wyatt suddenly seemed to get that this wasn't some cruel, made-up joke. It'd really happened. His face went from white as a ghost, to a horrible green color, and Stella wondered if he was going to throw up. She wouldn't blame him; her stomach was roiling uncontrollably, too.

Wyatt stood and began pacing back and forth across the kitchen. "You're not making any sense," he snapped. "Why the fuck would anyone gun down Bryce?" He stopped his pacing and fixed Tony with an uncompromising gaze.

The other man raised a thin eyebrow. "Because they thought he was you."

Wyatt reared away from Tony, as if he'd been struck, his face a grimace of fear and pain. "That's ridiculous. Why would anybody want to kill me?"

"It was only a matter of time before they came here," Tony mumbled, almost to himself. "I should've known better. Should never have gotten you involved."

Wyatt surged forward and grabbed Tony by the neck of his shirt. "What the fuck are you talking about? Who came here, and why? What does this have to do with me? What have you done, you bastard?" Wyatt shook Tony so hard his teeth rattled. Stella gave a squeak of surprise, frightened by his sudden violence.

"Wyatt," Levi cautioned. He was also on his feet, but he didn't intervene, he probably wanted answers as badly as Wyatt. Cat had also got to her feet and was standing stiff-legged beside Levi, as if ready for a fight.

"If you let me go, I'll tell you," Tony replied with a strangled gasp.

Wyatt gave a disgruntled snort but let go of Tony's shirt. "Start talking," he growled. He sat down heavily. Stella had never seen him look so fierce before. Suddenly, she caught a glimpse of what Wyatt may have looked like while he'd been in prison. This was no refined, cultured, well-behaved man. This was the primal, angry, and very determined warrior side of Wyatt. Most of her was appalled by the change in him, but a tiny part was also excited.

As if noticing her distress, he reached over and grabbed her hand. "I'm sorry. So sorry you had to be involved in any of this."

She squeezed his hand but said nothing, waiting for the wiry man at the end of the table to speak. Four pairs of eyes all turned toward Tony, and he shrunk back at the hostility in their stares. Stella had no idea who this man was, or what he meant to Wyatt. Even though she suspected he was a friend from prison, Wyatt had never substantiated her suspicions.

Tony spent some time rearranging his shirt, shooting a dagger-like glare at Wyatt from beneath lowered brows.

"First, have you still got my package?" he finally asked.

Wyatt scowled, and Stella wondered if he might grab him by the collar again, but he eventually said, "Of course. It's in my bedroom."

"You kept it on the premises? I thought you said you hid it?" Tony's voice was a mixture of scorn and concern.

"I did, then you told me you wanted it back, but you never turned up. Remember?" Wyatt's dark eyes glittered dangerously.

"Yeah, yeah." Tony waved a hand dismissively. "And I'll tell you the reason I didn't show up. But can I see my package first? It'll help answer some of your questions."

Wyatt glanced at Levi, who nodded. He cast another quick scowl in Tony's direction before he disappeared down the hallway.

Tony shifted in his seat, giving Levi a sideways glance. He had the look of a fidgety rat, on the constant lookout for danger. "Make it quick, will ya? I need to get outta here. Actually, youse all need to get outta here, if you know what's good for ya." For the first time that night, Tony's gaze landed on Stella, including her in his remark.

What the hell did he mean by that? Surely, she wasn't in any danger. Was she? She didn't have time to dissect that idea, however, as Wyatt returned, carrying a small, black backpack.

He dumped it on the table in front of Tony and said, "Here. Is this what's causing all the problems?"

"Don't tell me you haven't even taken a peek inside?" Tony's mouth dropped open.

"You told me not to. You said it'd be better for my health if I didn't know what was in there."

"Yeah, but I didn't think you'd actually listen to me."

Stella was enthralled as she watched Tony take out a bulky package wrapped in brown paper. He unwrapped it in front of them, spreading the layers of paper out on the tabletop as he went. More and more paper was unravelled, and Stella was beginning to wonder if there was actually anything inside, when a small, velvet bag was at last revealed. Tony held the bag in his hand, bouncing it on his palm as if gauging the weight.

"Feels like it's all still here," he announced, to no one in particular.

"Come on, open it up," Cat snarled, her patience finally wearing out. They all watched as Tony untied the drawstring and upended the bag onto the paper spread out on the table.

Stella sucked in a breath and then held it. *Merde.*

Diamonds.

Lots and lots of diamonds. Even in the dull light of the kitchen, they sparkled and glistened with a life of their own. What was Tony doing with all these diamonds?

CHAPTER EIGHT

"Holy fuck, are they what I think they are?" Cat was the first to speak.

"Yep, they're A-grade diamonds. Most of them cut, some uncut." Tony looked so fucking pleased with himself. But all Wyatt wanted to do was smash that grin right off his face, and whack those diamonds off the table, as if they never existed.

He had a horrible, sinking feeling. "Do they belong to who I think they do?" he asked heavily.

The pleased look on Tony's face evaporated, and his eyes darted around the room again.

"If you mean Dmytro, then no, the diamonds are mine."

"Bullshit." Wyatt's word was an explosion.

"They are." Tony looked up, but wouldn't meet Wyatt's gaze. "I took them as payment. He fucking owes me. How many times have I fenced his stolen goods for him? He never paid me properly, not once. This is supposed to be my retirement plan." Tony stood up, legs akimbo and eyebrows bristling belligerently.

"Holy shit, Tony." Wyatt couldn't find the words to express his disgust and dismay. He shook his head slowly. Not only had Tony stolen these diamonds, he'd dragged Wyatt into his stupid, scatterbrained idea.

"I didn't think he'd miss them. They're a small part of the rest of the haul. Dmytro wanted me to sell them on the black market. I told him prices were down right now. Global downturn, that kind of thing. And people were wary of buying his stuff, because he's doing time, and all that."

"So, you stole his gems and concocted some story, then ran off and gave them to me? Why did you do that?" The whole thing was mind-boggling, and Wyatt couldn't wrap his mind around the whole clusterfuck that was Tony and his diamonds. Now Tony's problem had become his problem.

Cat reached out, as if to pick up one of the diamonds, and Tony slapped her hand away.

Immediately, she was up on his face. "Don't you touch me." Her menacing growl even had Wyatt wanting to take a step back. He'd always loved that Cat was tough enough to take care of herself. Levi had done well to find a feisty woman who loved him as much as she did.

"Well, don't touch my diamonds then," Tony replied. It seemed Tony did have a backbone when it came to protecting his valuables.

Wyatt was still unclear as to Tony's motivations for including him in his harebrained scene. "Let me get this right. Dmytro figured out you took some of his diamonds, and now he's after you? Is that correct? And so, you gave me the diamonds, to what? Throw him off the trail?"

"Something like that," Tony agreed, still keeping an eagle eye on Cat, who'd retreated to lean against the kitchen countertop, scowling at him. Perhaps it was the oblivious way Tony seemed to wave away his question, or perhaps it was the fact that he was now in deadly danger because of this prick, but Wyatt suddenly saw red.

"You bastard. We were supposed to be friends. I just got out of jail. You only got out a month before me. Why would you do something like that to yourself? To me? You know I need to stay straight."

Tony looked at him, surprised. "I did it because we *are* friends. Friends are supposed to have each other's backs. I would've done the same for you."

Wyatt had heard enough from the slimy little sleazeball. Tony's version of friendship was warped and completely wrong. How could Wyatt have ever thought they'd been friends? He launched himself at Tony, and they fell into a sprawling heap on the kitchen floor. Vaguely, he thought he heard Stella scream as he punched Tony, but he was too incensed to stop.

Wyatt aimed a few punches at Tony's face, and the other man landed a good left hook into his ribs before Levi roared, "Stop it." He reached into the fray and dragged Wyatt off Tony. "We don't have time for this. You can sort out you warped version of *friendship* later." Levi was panting nearly as heavily as Wyatt. "You need to come up with some kind of plan, brother. Because I'm thinking those guys who killed Bryce will probably find their way here, soon. Am I right?" Levi snarled at Tony, who was levering himself off the floor, holding his nose with one hand.

"I thing you broke my gnose," Tony said, his words indistinct, as he tried to stem the flow of blood.

"Am I right?" Levi repeated, ignoring the other man's pain.

"Yeah. You're right. Now gan I have a nissue, or something?"

Cat flicked him a clean dishcloth from out of a drawer, still looking at him with disdain, as if she, too, wanted to punch him in the face. Stella was standing in the corner, hands covering her mouth, watching the entire scene unfold with wide-eyed horror. God, what must she think of all this?

"How long have we got?" Wyatt asked, feeling defeated

and exhausted.

"How the hell should I gnow?" Tony's voice was muffled behind the dishcloth. But when Wyatt took a menacing step toward him, he added, "If they had this address, they would've come here first, so they're going to need to ask around. But it won't take them long. We might have an hour, perhaps?"

An eerie silence descended on the little kitchen as they all digested Tony's words.

"Holy shit," Cat whispered into the stillness.

"You have to disappear for a while," Levi said coolly. "Give Tony back his diamonds, and you vanish into the woods. It's what you're good at. You can come back when all this has blown over."

Wyatt considered his brother's words. It wasn't a bad idea. And with such short notice, it might be the only idea. He locked eyes with Stella. A million different emotions flickered over her face, none of which he could decipher. She must be terrified. It might be a good idea to get out of here. At least if he went, he'd take the danger with him.

"You might become suspect number one if you run," Cat said.

Wyatt hadn't even considered that aspect. But it was true, he was probably the first person the police would come looking for over Bryce's death, because he had a record. They'd all conveniently forget that he'd been innocent.

"There's not a lot I can do about that right now." He lifted shoulder. "Dmytro is a lot scarier than Sheriff Buchanan. I'll face him later."

It all came crashing down on him. How much he'd screwed everything up. How much he was hurting the only family he truly cared about. How he was about to lose something good. Because whatever might've been building between him and Stella was now dead and buried. She'd never have anything to do with him again.

Wyatt sat and lowered his head into his hands. "I can't believe I got you guys involved in this. I'm so sorry." His chest ached with the weight of his words. The weight of what he'd brought onto his family. If only he hadn't ended up in jail. If only he hadn't tried to help his next-door neighbor, Zoe, in the first place. If only he'd seen Tony for the person he really was in prison.

Levi laid a hand on his shoulder. "I can't say I'm all that happy about it. And we're going to have a very long conversation when this is all over. But you know we got your back, bro."

Stella came up as well and lay her hand on his arm, murmuring, "It's okay. It'll be okay."

Which it wouldn't, but Wyatt didn't have the strength to argue. Then it hit him. What about Stella? Was she in danger, too? How was he going to protect her?

His gaze flicked between Stella and Levi. His brother must've picked up on Wyatt's distress.

"I'll look after her." Levi said, his face grim but determined. "I'll take her somewhere safe, maybe out of the state while we sort this out."

"What? I'm not going anywhere." Stella's hand tightened on his arm. Wyatt looked up. Everyone was staring at her. "You're not taking me anywhere," she repeated when nobody answered her.

"I'll do it." Cat squared her shoulders and tilted her chin toward Stella. "I'll take her on my motorcycle, they won't catch us on that. You should stay here," she said to Levi. "Wyatt will need someone on the ground who can give him feedback, let him know what's going on. Someone he trusts. And you're in the service; they'll tell you more than any of us."

"Why is no one listening to me?" Stella thumped the table

with her fist. "I'm. Not. Going. Anywhere," she repeated succinctly. "I'll be safe enough at Stargazer."

Tony spoke up for the first time in a while, one hand still covering his nose. "I hate to say it, but gno, you won't. Dmytro will hunt you down. He gnows about you. He'll use you to get to him." His gaze shot in Wyatt's direction as he dabbed at the blood trickling from his nose.

"How the hell does Dmytro know about Stella?" Wyatt felt the boiling anger in his gut flare again at Tony's words.

Tony shrunk back, then gave a half-hearted shrug. "It was the only way I could get away from his henchmen. They cornered me in Missoula yesterday. Anton Babich was with them." Tony shuddered as he said the name. "I had to give them something, or they would've tortured me."

Wyatt had heard the name before. He was Dmytro's top hitman, if the rumors were to be believed. Wyatt wasn't scared of a rumor, and it disgusted him that Tony had talked so easily.

Stella gasped beside him, as if she couldn't believe what she was hearing.

"And you what? Told them I had the diamonds? Is that how they found out I worked at CJ's, too?"

The wiry man nodded, sensing it was better not to speak.

"So, you're the reason Bryce is dead?" Wyatt ground out between gritted teeth. Tony had the courtesy to look sheepish. He took a step backward, away from the dark hatred Wyatt knew must be gleaming in his eyes. "I'm going to kill you." Wyatt hurled himself at Tony for the second time, driving him back against the countertop. It felt good to be using his fists, pounding the other man's flesh over and over. This time, his anger was cold and clear and pure. Tony wasn't fighting back, however, he was merely trying to protect himself from Wyatt's fury. It was Stella's scream that broke through the fog of fury motivating Wyatt. He backed away from the smaller man, who was now cowering in the corner of the kitchen.

"Leave him be," Levi said, standing in front of Wyatt and using his body as a shield to stop him from getting at Tony. "He's not worth it. And if what he said is true, you needed to be out of here ten minutes ago. And you're going to have to take Stella with you." They both looked over at Stella.

"But I don't want to go," Stella said in a small voice, her eyes filling with tears.

He went up and took both her hands in his. "I know you don't. I don't want to go, either. But we haven't got a choice. If we stay here, Dmytro's men will find us."

"What if we just give the diamonds back?" She was staring up into his face, looking hopeful. She had such long eyelashes; how had he never noticed that before?

"Oh, such a lovely, naïve little girl," Tony said sarcastically from his corner. "Sure. I'll just hand over the diamonds, shall I? Then everything will be fine? Is that right?"

"Well, won't it?" she asked, pulling her hands away from Wyatt so she could face Tony, swiping at a stray tear as she did so.

"Let me tell you some simple facts of life." Tony sounded defeated. He was still hunched over, leaning on the countertop. But there was determination in his eyes. "Dmytro wants his diamonds back, that's true. But he's also a man who values loyalty over just about everything else. It won't be enough for him to have his precious stash back. I've betrayed him, so he'll never let me live. And from his point of view, Wyatt has betrayed him, too."

"Oh... I didn't know." The hopeful look vanished from Stella's eyes.

"Of course, you didn't." Tony stood up straight, wincing a little and feeling at his ribs. "Which is why I'm coming with you."

It took a second for his words to sink in. "The hell you

are." Wyatt raised his fists, ready to take another round with the man.

"It's not a bad idea." Levi's words surprised Wyatt. "That way, at least you know he's not ratting you out. Again." Levi glared at Tony. "You'll be able to monitor him, and the diamonds, while we come up with a plan on how to get the jewels back to Dmytro and save your skin at the same time."

"He's not coming with us," Wyatt growled.

Cat stepped in between them. "You guys need to stop talking and get on with it." She stood with hands-on hips. "This arguing is getting you nowhere. What will you need to survive out there for the next few days? Come on, Wyatt, think."

"She's right," Levi agreed.

Wyatt's brain shifted gear painfully. He needed to start collecting camping gear and supplies so they could get out of here.

Sella was standing near the stove, glaring at him. "You can't be serious. We can't go out there. It's winter. It's freezing. We'll freeze to death."

"I've done this plenty of times," he reassured her. "I know what I'm doing."

"Yes, but I haven't." She came and got right up in his face. "And I've already told you, I don't want to go."

"Ooh, she's got guts, this one," Tony said.

"Shut up," they both replied in unison and then turned to look each other. Her tight frown relaxed a little, and the corners of her mouth turned up.

"You start packing," Cat said, stepping toward Stella. "I'll convince your lady, here, she has no other choice."

Wyatt spent the next ten minutes rushing around the house, pulling out his trusty old backpack, and then finding Levi's spare one. If Tony wanted to come with them, then he'd damn well have to carry a backpack. He wouldn't make

Stella carry it; he was already worried enough about her. There was only one tent small enough for them to carry while hiking, which he shoved at the bottom of his bag. Then he hunted out three sleeping bags, a first aid kit, matches and some freeze-dried food. Cat came into the living room while he was stuffing all these things into his backpack, and dumped a load of warm clothing in a pile next to him.

"Stella and I are pretty much the same size. She's going to need these, if she wants to stay warm and dry."

"Thanks, Cat." Words couldn't express how much he was in her and Levi's debt. There was a thick, knitted sweater; which he didn't think he'd ever seen Cat wearing. A pair of ski pants, a lightweight, thermal sweater, some woolen socks, and a proper pair of ski gloves, for which he was grateful. The thin knitted mittens Stella had on now wouldn't see her through a bitterly cold, winter's night.

Stella came in and sat in the winged chair, watching everything with an air of disbelief. He knew he was expecting a lot of her, but they really had no other choice, and he hoped she'd pull herself out of her funk soon. He was going to need her to be focused and aware for the trek into the mountains tonight. His heart wept for her. With her hands between her knees and her face pale, she looked so young and fragile; like a child waiting to be told what to do. Sudden realization hit him. Stella was going to be relying on him, and him alone, to get her through. It was his fault she was here, and now she was being forced to run for her life.

This was the whole reason Wyatt never wanted to get involved with anyone else. He was bad news. He'd tried hard to make things better, to put his life back on the right path. Maybe he was cursed. Whatever it was, there was something dark and sinister inside him. He didn't deserve to be surrounded by people who cared about him. Once this was over, he'd move away. Go somewhere he couldn't hurt the people he loved.

Tony sat in another chair, also watching proceedings. The bastard could've offered to help. But then, Wyatt preferred to do it himself; at least he'd know it was done properly.

"What about him?" Wyatt tilted his chin in Tony's direction. He didn't want to provide the betrayer with anything, but it'd do no good if Tony couldn't even make it through the first night because he was freezing to death.

Cat lifted a corner of her mouth in a snarl, but turned on her heel and headed to the bedroom to get some of Levi's warm clothes for him.

"I've got something else you're going to need," Levi called, and then disappeared outside. Wyatt continued to shove items into his backpack, and Levi returned a minute later, holding a satellite phone. "Here, take this. It's my spare, and it's the best way to communicate."

"I can't take this, isn't that against regulations? I don't want to get you in trouble."

"I'll get a new one. I'll say I broke this one; it happens all the time."

His brother stared at him, and Wyatt stared back. Levi was his kid brother, but here he was looking after him. Levi had been doing great with his new job and getting engaged. And now, Wyatt had come along and fucked it up for him.

Wyatt wanted to put his head back in his hands, make this all go away. Instead, he said, "Thank you."

"Make sure you keep your own cell phones turned off," Levi added, as he handed the sat phone to Wyatt. "That way, no one can track you."

Wyatt nodded. "We're going to walk to the old abandoned house out on Black Pine Ridge Road. Do you know where it is?"

Wyatt had found the house while out hiking a few months back. It had an aura of sadness about it, a place where

72

humanity had failed. But something about it felt important, as well. A week later, he'd tried to find it by driving there. It'd taken him a few wrong turns and switchbacks, but he'd finally found his way. He'd been back a few times since, when he needed to get away for a night; needed some solitude or a place to think. And when he needed to hide some stolen diamonds. It was the perfect place to meet up with Levi in a few days.

Levi cocked his head. "You mean the one near Apache Gulch?"

"Yep, that's it. We'll take the trail over the Butte Cabin Ridge." It was about a forty mile-hike. He could do it in two days, but in winter, with two inexperienced people to lead, and most of the trails closed, it'd probably take them three. "If the coast is clear, we'll see you at the old house in three days' time. I'll call you on the sat phone."

"And if it's not...?"

No one answered that question.

CHAPTER NINE

An icy wind bit into Stella's cheeks. It was so quiet out here; the only sound was that of their footsteps crunching in the snow. A night bird called somewhere in the distance. She had no idea what type of bird it was. And why would she? She knew nothing about these forests, or this wilderness. And yet here she was, traipsing up a trail behind Wyatt in the pitch dark.

She wrapped the scarf Wyatt gave her tighter around her neck, dipping her chin into the softness of the yarn to keep warm.

This entire night was absolutely crazy. Her mother had been right, she should never have left France. She should never have agreed to have dinner with Wyatt. Should have left well enough alone and stayed at the ranch, like the good girl that she was.

Tony was behind her; she heard his footsteps and his rasping breath. It was all his fault. At first, when Wyatt attacked Tony back in the kitchen, she'd been appalled. She'd never witnessed such violence before. But after Tony revealed the extent of his betrayal, and Wyatt had started punching him a second time, Stella had wanted to join in. This man was nothing but a snake; a wicked, slithering, snake. He shouldn't be calling himself Wyatt's friend.

They were walking without flashlights; Wyatt said it'd be better if their eyes adjusted to the dark, then their night-vision would kick in, and they'd see much better. Stella had thought he was crazy, but twenty minutes into the trek, her surroundings were becoming clearer. She could see Wyatt's footprints, dark holes in the lighter snow. And the surrounding forest, which'd been an impenetrable, pitch black, was now transforming so she could see individual trunks and the branches of the fir trees rising to meet the cold stars above.

"The trail will go up soon as we climb into the foothills." Wyatt said, breaking the silence that'd descended over the trio. At least he knew where he was going, which was a minor comfort. Although, how he could tell which direction they were heading in the dark was beyond her.

"Oh, goodie," Tony said sarcastically from the rear.

Wyatt stopped in his tracks and turned around. "You can go back any time you like. We don't want you here."

Tony held up his hands, as if in surrender. "Yeah, yeah, sorry."

After a few seconds, Wyatt continued walking. He had a large backpack slung across his shoulders, and Tony was carrying a smaller one. Stella had watched the snake stow the little bag of diamonds securely at the bottom of his backpack. Such a small thing, to be worth so much money. It still boggled Stella's mind. It was surreal, like she was in the middle of a bad dream and would wake up at any second, warm and snug in her bed, back at Stargazer.

Cat had given her a pair of hiking boots and some thick socks. Said she'd bought them a year ago, but hardly ever used them. She preferred her steel-toed work boots she wore in the workshop; she even hiked in them, which was so much like Cat, Stella had to laugh. The two of them were the same size, which was a blessing. The boots would make this hike into the wilderness a little more bearable. She just hoped they remained a perfect fit, and she didn't end up with blisters on her heels.

She perceived, rather than saw, the ground slope upward; her thighs burned and her breath became labored. Silence surrounded them, almost as thick as the black night. It was time she asked some of the questions that were boiling through her brain. If she was doing this, she needed to understand exactly what was happening.

"Where are we going?" she said to Wyatt's back. "I need to know what your plan is."

He glanced over his shoulder but didn't stop walking. "There's a spot high in the foothills that'll make a good campsite. We can halt there for the night."

Stella almost laughed out loud. "You mean, for what's left of the night." It was already midnight.

"Yeah," he replied, an apology in his voice. "But if we can get a few hours away from Stevensville, it'll make us much safer. No one should find us, up here."

Stella raised her eyebrows at that, but he was probably right. No sane person would head into the mountains on a cold winter's night. If these bad men actually existed—and Stella was still dubious about that bit, surely, it was just another tall tale Tony was telling to get Wyatt to do what he wanted; she didn't trust that man as far as she could throw him—they'd be looking for them out on the roads, back in civilization, not here in the middle of nowhere.

"Why wouldn't you let me call Penny? Or Joseph? He'll be so mad when I don't turn up tomorrow morning." Her first instinct when Cat had convinced her there was no other option than for her to trek into the wilderness with Wyatt, was to reach for her phone. But Wyatt had covered the screen with his hand and shook his head, his eyes sympathetic but also implacable. Stella also had thoughts of calling her mother, to tell her she was going to be out of touch for a few days. Or at the very least, call Aunt Celeste, spin some story so they wouldn't worry.

Levi had made sure they'd all turned their cells off before they left the house. Stella considered those stories about the bad guys being able to track people through their phones to only be true in the movies. But Levi shook his head. "If this Dmytro is as big a player in the crime syndicates as Tony is making him out to be, rest assured, he'll be able to find you. These gangs sometimes have technology that even the police don't have," Levi had said. Stella stared at him, still disbelieving, but his dark eyes had been so sure, she'd been convinced, and the conversation had ended with Stella putting her phone—now switched off—into the bottom of Wyatt's pack.

"The fewer people who have knowledge of where we are, the better," Wyatt said now, puffing a little as the trail got steeper.

"But what will they think of me?" Stella continued, her voice wavering slightly. She hated to let anyone down. She had a strict work ethic, was never sick, and hardly ever took a day off. "I always thought it was better to let people know when you were trekking into the wilderness."

"Cat and Levi know where we are; that's enough, for now. And they'll pass the details on to Dean. He should be aware anyway, just in case these guys turn up at the ranch. But he'll tell Joseph and Penny that you're spending a couple of days with me."

"*Zut*," she said impatiently, stopping on the trail and kicking at a clump of snow. "But won't they be under the impression I'm some kind of…loose woman, who goes off with the first man she meets?"

"No, they won't. They should know you better than that.

Hell, even I realize you wouldn't do that, and I've only known you a week," Wyatt replied.

"Is that all?" Tony interrupted. "The way you look at her, I was sure it was true love."

"Shut up, Tony, or I'll leave you behind."

Tony wisely quietened down.

"Do you trust me?" Wyatt asked. He stopped and turned around, searching her face in the dark for an answer.

That was an interesting question. On the surface, she trusted him. He had saved her from the wreck on Christmas Eve. After their time spent huddled in the truck together, she felt like she was familiar with him. But was she really? How well could you know someone after only one night? Stella delved a little deeper into her mixed thoughts and emotions. Did she trust this man with the piercing, dark eyes, and solemn features?

Not surprisingly, her answer was a resounding yes. She lifted her chin. "I guess I do." It was hard to determine his exact features in the starlight, but his lips finally curled into a smile.

"Yeah, well, I'm not sure I do," Tony interrupted.

"I don't care what you think. And you'd do well *not* to trust me at this stage," Wyatt snarled. He turned his gaze back to Stella. He was tall and solid, standing above her on the trail, the bulk of the backpack and his thick coat making him look even more imposing.

"I might not be the brightest social butterfly, I'm not good at parties, and I might not have the smarts to be a lawyer or doctor, but I am good at this. I know how to survive in the wilderness. I will keep us safe."

How could she argue with that? "Okay," she said simply.

He turned around, as if satisfied with her answer, and they kept walking. They walked and walked. Sometimes the snow got deeper, and then Wyatt would have to wade through it, forging a trail for them to follow. At other times, there was a break in the forest canopy and Stella could see the stars so high above them. She began to sweat inside her coat as her breath came in quick puffs. The terrain was getting steeper, and she was worried if she missed a step, she might tumble backward all the way down the hill.

"Are we there yet?" Tony huffed from behind her, not quite loud enough for Wyatt to hear, more for her ears only.

She ignored him, but that the same question had been niggling at her, too. Then, as if the gods had been listening, she crested a small rise behind Wyatt and came into a small, level clearing.

"This is it," Wyatt said, dropping his backpack on the ground.

"Great," said Tony, also dropping his backpack and leaning on his knees to get his breath back.

"Stella can have the tent, you and I will sleep under the stars," Wyatt announced.

"You got to be kidding," Tony spluttered.

"I've only got one tent. I'll build a fire to keep us warm. We'll be fine." Wyatt was already undoing his backpack.

"What about bears? Or wolves? I'm not sleeping out in the open, exposed." Tony stood up straight, his eyes casting around the small clearing as if a bear were about to jump out at any second.

His words startled Stella; she hadn't even thought about unfriendly wildlife.

"Don't be stupid, Tony. The bears are all hibernating, it's the middle of winter."

Tony's face cleared a little. And Stella drew in a deep breath. Of course, the bears were hibernating, everyone knew that. Even with her limited knowledge of this mountainous forest, she should've remembered that kind of detail. This whole mad dash in the middle of night was confusing her brain so she couldn't think straight anymore.

"What about wolves? I'm sure I heard a wolf howling, earlier." Tony still wasn't convinced.

Wyatt stopped unpacking. "Look, it's either that, or you walk back down to Stevensville, and find yourself a nice warm hotel room. Perhaps you could use a credit card, make it easier for Dmytro's hitman to find you." He glared at Tony.

Tony said nothing more, but Stella could feel the irritation oozing off him. Wyatt needed to be more careful with his complete disregard for Tony's feelings, making his disgust for the man so evident. This man was putting up with Wyatt because he was afraid of what was following him. But he might only be prepared to put up with so much before he retaliated. Tony had kept up with them on the hike—Stella knew Wyatt had been taking it slow for her sake—but even though the other man looked thin and wiry, she'd heard his breath rasping in his throat all the way up the hill. He didn't sound very fit. Would he balk at a longer, harder climb? Wyatt might've made a big mistake bringing Tony along with them.

She also didn't like the way Tony looked at her. The way his eyes flicked up and down her legs when he thought she wasn't looking. Even now, in the dark of the night forest, she could feel his gaze on her. It made her shiver.

Stella said nothing, however, and she felt a little useless as she watched Wyatt move efficiently around the clearing. First, he used his feet and sometimes his gloved hands to clear the snow away, forming a small circle. The snow wasn't deep beneath the trees. They hadn't had any more snowfall since the blizzard a week ago. It'd had settled and some of it'd melted, leaving a hard, icy crust on top.

Then Wyatt took out a bag that looked way too small to contain a tent. But when he shook it out, the fine, parachute-like material expanded into a tent big enough for two people.

He erected the little tent quickly. She'd never set up a tent in her life. But she hated to be powerless or ignorant, and decided to remedy that. In the morning, when it was light and she could see what he was doing, she'd ask Wyatt to show her how. Then Wyatt walked over to the nearest pine tree and broke off some smaller branches, ending up with an armful of pine needles. Scattering them on the floor of the tent, he stood up and said, "That'll help keep you a little warmer, if you're not sleeping directly on the ground."

Stella nodded. It made sense, but she would never in a million years have thought of that, herself.

Tony leaned against a tree trunk a few feet away, watching her and Wyatt, but doing nothing to help.

"If you want to stay warm tonight, you need to collect some wood," Wyatt said to Tony.

The other man grunted, but pushed away from the tree and walked off into the forest. She could hear him crashing around in dark.

Once Tony was gone, Stella whispered, "Share the tent with me, please. I'll feel safer if you're inside."

Wyatt stopped what he was doing. "Really? Are you sure? I didn't want to…" He let the rest of his sentence trail away.

Stella had been thinking merely about safety when she made the suggestion. But now, she remembered their time spent together in his truck and their kiss tonight, and a fizz of something else ran through her.

She nodded slowly.

"It'll definitely be warmer if we both share the tent," he said into the awkward silence.

"Yes, I'm sure," she replied. She wondered what Tony might think and then decided she didn't care. Instead, she asked, "Do you trust Tony? To leave him outside by himself, I mean? What if he tries to run away, or something?"

"No, I don't trust him. But he'd be stupid to leave in the

middle of the night. He'd get lost."

That was true, but it wasn't necessarily what she meant. She couldn't see Wyatt's features in the dim light, but he cocked his head, understanding her unasked question.

He moved in closer so he could whisper in her ear. "Don't worry, I have insurance, if he should try anything…dodgy." Wyatt patted his coat pocket. "I have a weapon. Levi gave me his spare 22 pistol. It's small, but it's better than nothing." His breath was warm on the side of her neck. Stella wasn't sure if this news reassured her, or terrified her. Because it made it that much more real.

But then something even scarier occurred to her. "Do you think Tony's got a gun, too?"

CHAPTER TEN

Wyatt tilted his head toward the stars and thought for a second. "I don't think so. I would've felt it when we were fighting. He might have had one stashed in his car, but that's why we wouldn't let him go back outside." Wyatt wasn't sure if this was a good thing or not. Being unarmed may well make Tony feel more vulnerable, and therefore more desperate.

The sound of Tony returning cut off any further conversation. Dumping an armload full of branches, he said with disgust, "There you go, Mr. Boy Scout. Now light a damn fire, I'm fucking freezing."

Wyatt decided not to comment, but went about clearing another spot in the snow. "If you could find some small, dry twigs, that'd be helpful," he said quietly to Stella. He watched her from the corner of his eye as he continued to clear the area with his gloved hands. He could tell she dare not go too far into the forest, instead, stopping at a fallen log near the edge of the clearing, which had some dead branches pointing out toward the sky. Returning, she handed her fistful of twigs to Wyatt. He already had a few pieces of shredded paper in a small pile, and he added her twigs, then set a match to it. The wood was damp and cold from the snow, but as he slowly added more twigs, the meager fire grew. Tony stood on the other side, holding out his hands to capture the warmth.

"I brought the rest of the hot chocolate in the Thermos, do you want some?" Wyatt asked Stella.

She paused for a second, as if surprised, and he wondered if she was thinking the same thing he was. Had their dinner-date really only been a few hours ago? It felt like forever. His life had changed in those few seconds after Tony arrived. Both their lives had altered. Hot chocolate sounded so normal, so mundane. Something you'd drink at home by the fire. Not while you were on the run from a group of crazed gunmen.

"I'll have some," Tony interjected. Wyatt ignored him.

"Yes, please," she said, shooting a quick glance in Tony's direction.

"Why don't you hop into your sleeping bag, so you stay warm. I'll get Tony organized, then I'll bring it to you."

She nodded gratefully. It'd be darker in the tent, but the firelight should cast enough radiating light through the fabric to see by. Wyatt had laid out two sleeping bags, side-by-side. There were no mattresses and no pillows, as it was all he could carry. Stella had been skeptical when he'd first unpacked the sleeping bags. He'd told her they were special bags, made for hiking; they were lightweight and packed down to small size, but very warm. He also suggested she sleep fully clothed, keeping her coat on. If she got too hot during the night, she could always take it off, but somehow, he thought she was going to need every scrap of clothing she had on to stay warm. She'd already swapped her beautiful pink sweater for Cat's more practical, knitted one and had changed into Cat's ski pants, as well. He didn't tell her the other reason not to get undressed was in case they had to leave quickly.

Wyatt had borrowed one of Levi's camping bags, and he

helped Tony unroll it and place it next to the fire in the spot he'd cleared. He should spread the ground with dry leaves, the same as he had for Stella and himself as insulation, but he couldn't be bothered. Tony was going to be cold, but if he kept the fire well-stoked, he'd survive the night. Wyatt had measured the practical need for a fire versus the slim chance of someone following them. If that were the case, it'd act as a beacon calling them in. He decided that the fire outweighed the very low risk that someone else was out here. He didn't think even Dmytro's hitman would be clever enough to figure out where they'd gone. If they had worked out he'd run into the mountains, there were so many trails, it'd take days for them to figure out which way they'd gone.

After filling a pan with snow to melt by the fire—it'd need to be filtered in the morning before they could pour it into their drink bottles—Wyatt thrust a half-full cup of hot chocolate at Tony. He was loath to give the man anything, but it wasn't worth listening to his moaning all night if he didn't.

"Remember to keep the fire stoked. There's plenty of wood over there." While Stella was getting settled, he'd forced Tony to accompany him back into the forest and find more wood to feed the fire throughout the night.

"Yeah, thanks for nothing, dude."

Wyatt wanted to swing around and punch him in the face. Ungrateful sod. Instead, he took the Thermos and two more cups, and went to join Stella. She was tucked up in her sleeping bag, a bulky shape in the dim confines of the tent. He handed her the Thermos and the cups, and then crawled in beside her, careful to knock the snow off his boots as he did so. He removed his boots and left them in the little vestibule at the front of the tent, next to Stella's.

"This is so good," Stella practically hummed the words, handing him a cup of hot chocolate once he'd settled into his sleeping bag.

"I know. I nearly left it behind, because I wasn't sure I needed the extra weight. But we can also brew some coffee in the morning to drink on our hike tomorrow. It'll help keep us warm."

They sat in silence for a few moments, listening to the sounds of Tony getting settled and sipping from their plastic mugs.

"What about Cat and Levi? Will they be safe, if they stay in their house?"

He'd been wondering how long it would take for her to figure out the other two were in danger. She must've been mulling over a few things in her head as she sat getting warm in the tent.

"We don't know," Wyatt replied. "But Levi won't take any chances, regardless. They're going to stay at Stargazer for the next little while, just to be on the safe side." He, Levi, and Cat had discussed it quickly in the kitchen before they left. Stella had been preoccupied, staring out the window, trying to come to terms with everything that was happening. Levi had seemed to know what he was going to say, even before he opened his mouth.

"Don't worry about us," he'd said, laying a hand on Wyatt's shoulder. "I realize the danger. But Cat and I can take care of ourselves. We'll keep our eyes and ears open. You know I'd never let anything happen to Cat."

Cat had snorted at his words, but the look she threw him contained a mixture of exasperation and unending love. Wyatt hoped he could find a woman who'd love him as deeply as Cat loved Levi. Was Stella that woman? He shook his head and concentrated on rest of Levi's words, acknowledging that Stargazer was the best place to be, and they should head there tonight, as soon as Wyatt and his little troupe left.

Wyatt wiggled deeper into the sleeping bag. His toes were

at last warming up.

Seeming to accept his explanation, Stella asked another question. "How do we know this person—what's his name?"

"Dmytro," Wyatt supplied.

"Yes, Dmytro. How do we know those men he sent to get the diamonds won't follow us into the mountains?"

"We don't," Wyatt answered quietly. "But they'll have to be pretty damn good, to find us out here. I'm not even sure my brother could find us, and he knows where we're going."

"Where are we going, exactly?" Stella finished her cupful and put it aside, then snuggled down into her bag.

"We're headed for a ruined house. It's on the other side of this range; a two-day hike from here." A tight knot formed in his stomach. Should he tell her? It was probably too late to keep it a secret now, she knew everything else. "It's where I originally hid Tony's diamonds. I was coming back from there on the day I rescued you."

"Really?" Stella sounded genuinely surprised. He waited for the disgust and disdain he knew he was due. She had every right to get mad at him. "That was kind of lucky, don't you think?"

"What?" Her comment took him by surprise.

"In some twisted kind of way, we can thank Tony for our first meeting."

It was true, but not the way he would've preferred to meet Stella. "I guess so," he agreed.

Stella yawned. She was lying flat now. He lay down next to her, and could just make out the pale oval of her face beneath her knit cap, the bag tucked up under her chin.

"Wyatt?" she breathed.

"Hmm."

"I know this probably isn't the time or the place. I was going to tell you earlier. And well... I think you should know." She had his attention, even if she seemed to be hedging around whatever it was she wanted to say. "Armand and I broke up yesterday."

"Really?" Dozens of questions had sprung to mind. Had she left him, or did he leave her? Was her heart broken? But if her tone was anything to go by, she seemed to be untroubled by it all. She had mentioned they were having problems. Was it because of him? No, that was being plain big-headed. He settled on asking, "Are you okay about it?"

"Yes, I think so." She smothered a yawn. "I'm sorry, I'm too tired to talk more, but I wanted you to know."

"Thank you. Let me know if you get too cold," he said.

"I will." She yawned again, and soon he could hear the calm, regular breathing of someone in a deep sleep. Sleep would be a lot more elusive for him, however. His mind was going a million miles an hour, and not only about that bombshell regarding Armand.

Wyatt patted the bulge in his pocket, and it comforted him, even while he hoped to God he didn't have to use it.

* * *

Wyatt woke with a start. It took him a few seconds to realize where he was. Thin, morning light filtered through the material of the tent. Expelling a breath, he watched the steam from his mouth drift up to the ceiling.

He wasn't warm, exactly, but neither was he as cold as he might've expected after a night out in the forest. The reason for his comfort was snuggled on his left shoulder. At some time during the night, Stella must've rolled over and tucked herself in next to him, probably seeking his extra body heat. She still had her sleeping bag pulled up, almost covering her ears. He didn't remember doing it, but he'd thrown his arm over her shoulder sometime in the night, pulling her in closer. Even with the plastic floor of the tent and the pine needles beneath them, the cold had seeped up through the ground. But where they lay together, their sleeping bags entwined, he was surprisingly warm.

Wyatt thought back and tried to remember if he'd ever taken a girl out camping before. Nope, he'd never shared a tent with anyone else. Idly, he wondered why that was, because right now, it was decidedly cozy in here. He'd taken to camping out—or sleeping rough, as his dad called it— when he was around sixteen years old. He'd started withdrawing from his small family after his mother left, at the age of thirteen; to get away from his drunken father, mostly. But also, because he felt he couldn't breathe in that house anymore, as if it were less without his mother's warm presence to light it up. Much later, Wyatt had found out she'd returned to her hometown in Italy. But at the time, even though the logical part of his brain knew it wasn't true—he'd blamed himself. If he'd been a better son, perhaps she would've stayed.

Stella stirred beneath his arm, breaking his memories. She yawned, then snuggled in deeper to his chest, as if seeking the last of his heat. He smiled to himself at the thought she was no longer with Armand. She was a free woman. But exactly what that meant for him, Wyatt still had no idea.

"Were you warm enough?" he asked gently into the top of her knit cap.

"Hmm?" She hummed drowsily. "Not really," she admitted, voice thick with sleep. "But it wasn't as cold as I was expecting, either. Having my personal hot water bottle helped." She pushed back a little, so she could study his face.

He couldn't help it; she was so cute, all bundled up in the sleeping bag, her knit cap askew on her head, long drifts of hair escaping out the sides. He kissed the tip of her nose. Her green eyes darkened and fixed on him.

"What was that for?"

"I don't know. Because you look like a kid wrapped in your blankie." He used his finger to brush some strands away from her face, then ran it down the soft swell of her cheek. "But also, because you're so brave. You've hardly complained at all, after I dragged you into this mess. You've taken most of it in your stride, even though you're way out of your comfort zone."

She didn't answer, merely fixed those leaf-green eyes on his lips, letting him appreciate what she wanted.

As if she'd lassoed him with an elastic cord, his head was drawn toward her, and his mouth closed inexorably on hers. A sigh left her lips as they touched. Then she opened to him, and their kiss deepened. She tilted her head slightly to give him better access to her lips.

He wasn't sure if all French women were this good, but Stella was the best kisser he'd ever known. And he'd had his fair share. It was something about her inner sensuality, her own self-confidence as a strong, sexy woman. She gave back to him as an equal, not letting him dominate her, but not dominating him, either.

His cock stirred and hardened almost immediately, and he wished these layers of clothing and sleeping bags didn't exist. The only bit of skin available to him was her face and the side of her neck. He ran his fingers up under the back of her knit cap, then wrapped them around her slim neck and slid them beneath her scarf to find the dip beneath her collarbone.

"Hey." Tony's rough voice broke his warm bubble of desire.

Wyatt exhaled loudly.

"If you guys aren't awake yet, then you need to be. It's fucking freezing." The side of the tent shook, as if Tony had kicked it. Wyatt let out a grunt of irritation. When this was all over, he really was going to take great pleasure in slowly throttling Tony. The jerk.

Stella smiled up at him, a lopsided grin full of regret mixed with humor. "I suppose…"

"Yes," he murmured. "You stay here where it's warm, and I'll go and re-build the fire."

Stella considered his words. "No, I'll get up, too. I'm sure we need to get moving soon, don't we?"

He was surprised. She'd grasped the situation well. For a city girl, she was doing great. Better than Tony, that was for sure.

He and Levi had checked the weather forecast quickly before they'd left last night, and there was no snow predicted for the next few days, which was a blessing. At least they wouldn't be battling the elements along with everything else they had to contend with.

They had a full day of hiking ahead of them. Stella was right, she should get up now, too. It was still a long way over this range and then back down the other side, before they made it to the abandoned house. And even then, they had no clear plan. No obvious way out of this mess.

CHAPTER ELEVEN

By the time Stella crawled out of the tent, Wyatt had a small fire going. She went and stood next to him, hoping to warm her hands, giving Tony a quick nod of acknowledgement. Tony scowled at her. He didn't look happy; he had his arms crossed, and was stamping his feet on the ground, as if to thaw out. His face looked worse for wear, too. It'd been too dark to see it last night, but this morning she could see the evidence of Wyatt's brutality written all over him. Bruising was turning his left eye purple and there was a hint of dried blood around his nostrils, beneath a nose that was decidedly crooked. She winced. Wyatt sure had packed a punch.

It was cold out here, after the relative warmth of her sleeping bag, and she felt a tiny bit sorry for Tony. She was glad of the protection from the tent, as well as having Wyatt by her side last night. Tony must be frozen.

Dawn was creeping fingers of light into the sky, which was a pale, indigo blue, edging to subtle pink as the sun rose behind the mountains. Even though it was freezing, Stella could appreciate the calm serenity of the fresh, morning light. Everything was so still, she could hear a pin drop. She saw why Wyatt might prefer to camp outside. It was beautiful. There was a soft whoosh and then a thud, as a clump of snow slid off a branch and landed on the ground. The first time she heard that sound on the trek through the dark last night, she had no idea what it was. Wyatt had to explain it to her. A bird trilled its message to the morning. There were so many things she didn't understand about trekking in the wilderness, but even after only one night, she wanted to learn more.

Wyatt piled the remaining branches they'd gathered onto the fire.

"We'll need more wood," he said to Tony. Tony just glared at him and didn't budge, holding his hands above the flames. What an ass. She'd been about to ask him if he needed some painkillers for his face, but she changed her mind.

"I'll help," she said, and followed Wyatt into the dense forest. They didn't have to go far to find pieces of dead wood and she was glad of the exercise, as it warmed her up considerably.

"I'm checking in with Levi," Wyatt said, once they returned.

"Good. We need to know what's going on in town." It was the first bit of animation Tony had shown all morning, his face finally changing from that perpetual scowl.

Wyatt retrieved the sat phone from the top of his pack and turned it on. Then he dialed Levi's number. Both she and Tony listened to the one-sided conversation carefully. Wyatt's single-word responses frustrated Stella, giving her nothing. But his deepening frown told her what she suspected; it was bad news.

Finally, he ended the call, pursing his lips as he looked at her.

"Well?" Tony demanded.

Wyatt shot him a disapproving look. "It's pretty much as we expected. The entire town is in an uproar over Bryce's death. Everyone is anxious, frightened, demanding answers. There are a few vigilantes running around with shotguns, hoping to catch the killer."

"But it's so early in the morning," Stella said. "How did they…?"

"This is a small country town, gossip spreads like wildfire." Wyatt said, anticipating her question. "And something like this, a local being gunned down in his own diner, well, that's just about the biggest thing to have happened here in years."

Stella opened her mouth to reply, but Tony cut her off. "Yeah, yeah, I'm not interested in the town's crazy lunatics, I'm interested in whether Levi's heard anything more about Dmytro's men."

Wyatt took his time to tuck the satellite phone into his backpack before he turned to answer. Tony was getting more irritated with every passing second, but then she guessed it was exactly what Wyatt intended. Tony was rude and arrogant, and Stella wondered what'd ever possessed Wyatt to befriend him in the first place.

"Levi has heard nothing else. If it was Dmytro's men—"

"Of course it was Dmytro's men," Tony snapped.

"If it *was* Dmytro's men," Wyatt continued, as if Tony hadn't interrupted him, "then they've gone to ground, because there's no sign of them."

"What about the cops, what are they doing about it?" Tony demanded.

"Levi has a buddy in the sheriff's office, Jude, but even he won't say much. One thing he did tell him, though, is that my sudden departure is highly suspicious. Jude said they're issuing a warrant for my arrest today."

Stella gasped. It was just like Levi had predicted. He'd warned Wyatt something like this would happen.

"Oh, no. That's terrible. You had nothing to do with this." She took hold of his hand, an offer of comfort.

He shrugged, seeming to ignore her touch.

"I knew it would happen." There was a bitterness to his tone. "Once a felon, always felon."

"Yeah, sorry about that, man." For once Tony seemed to be sincerely apologetic.

"Don't give me that shit." Wyatt rounded on Tony. "This is all your fault. Bryce is dead because of you. And now I'm a wanted man because of you." Wyatt's face flushed red beneath his knit cap, and Stella wondered if he was going to punch the man again. She still had hold of his hand, and she squeezed it tight.

Wyatt drew in a deep breath, apparently deciding Tony wasn't worth it. "Let's make some breakfast and get out of here. We need to keep moving." But his fingers clasped hers tight for a few seconds before he let her go. It was heartening to see Wyatt control his temper. Even if it was just for her sake, she was grateful. From what she was learning about him, he was serious and solemn, but also thoughtful and sensitive.

He kept that compassionate side hidden from most people, perhaps another effect of spending time in jail with hardened criminals. But she knew it was there, and she hoped to see more of it.

Stella couldn't decide if Wyatt's decision to take her and Tony into the mountains to keep them safe was a good thing, or not. Disappearing like he had made him look guilty, and she could see why the police would jump to conclusions. But then again, perhaps it was a good thing Wyatt was out here, instead of being dragged to jail to be questioned and accused. From what she knew of Wyatt, it would do his injured soul no good to go through all that. Her heart ached for him. It seemed no matter which way he turned; the choices weren't good. He was in a dire situation, and she wasn't sure if there was anything she could do to help him. In fact, she was probably hindering him.

Wyatt took the pan he'd filed with snow last night and filled their water bottles through some sort of filtering device. Then he heated the rest over the fire until it boiled. They had a quick breakfast; a freeze-dried hiking meal; it might've been scrambled eggs. She ate quietly, and watched Wyatt make up the Thermos of coffee, then helped as he re-packed the sleeping bags and took down the tent. They were ready to go in less than fifteen minutes.

Since Wyatt's outburst, Tony had remained sullenly silent, which Stella thought was a good thing. Every time he opened his mouth, he either said something rude, or egotistical, or just plain stupid. She followed Wyatt as he led them away from their camp and up the mountainside.

* * *

Stella heard a noise. A subtle *ping*. She'd recognize that sound anywhere. It was the sound of a message notification on a cell phone. She saw Wyatt's head snap up as he heard it too. It was nearly lunchtime by Stella's guess, and they were climbing a steep section toward a high ridgeline. She had her head down, watching where she was putting her feet, using her hands to help now and then.

Wyatt swung around, just as Tony swore softly under his breath. His gaze bored into the smaller man below him on the trail.

"Tell me that wasn't your fucking cell," Wyatt ground out between clenched teeth.

"Fuck," Tony said as he reached into his back pocket and pulled out his phone. He jabbed repeatedly at the buttons and swore again.

"Tony." Wyatt's voice was dangerously cold.

"What?" Tony said belligerently. Then when he caught Wyatt staring at him, he admitted, "Yeah, I turned it on when we stopped for a break earlier, so what? There's no reception out here in these godforsaken mountains, anyway. I guess I forgot to turn it off."

"Do it. Right now." Wyatt descended the path, looking as if he were about to snatch the phone away from Tony. Stella stepped back to let him pass, her worried gaze finding his as he passed her by. Tony had turned the cell off by the time Wyatt reached him and tucked it away out of sight.

Stella stared at Tony in surprise. Hadn't he listened to what Levi told them back at the house? Surely, he understood there was a risk in using it? She hadn't touched her phone since she'd put in the backpack last night.

"Have you turned it on at any other time?" Wyatt asked quietly.

Tony shot him a guilty look.

She'd been feeling sorry for him because his face looked so sore, but Stella decided she'd never despised a man more than she did right now. Tony was a lying little weasel. Wyatt was trying to help him, and all he was doing was whining at every turn, then sabotaging their plans.

"Well?" Wyatt demanded.

"I checked it last night, after you were both cozy in your little love nest."

Stella watched Wyatt's shoulders tense.

"I need to know what's going on. There were ten missed calls from Dmytro, and—"

"Of course there were, he wants his diamonds back. And he wants to find you," Wyatt shouted. "I warned you Dmytro might be able to track us if you turned your phone on, you imbecile."

"It's off now," Tony said, with a sulky tilt to his mouth.

"Make sure it doesn't go on again, or I'll confiscate it." Wyatt stomped back up the trail.

Tony mumbled to himself, "I'd like to see you try."

She ignored the loathsome man and began walking, but a shiver of foreboding ran up her spine.

CHAPTER TWELVE

Wyatt's anger slowly ebbed until it was a dull simmering in his belly. When he'd heard Tony's cell phone earlier today, he'd been ready to punch a tree. The only thing that'd stopped him was Stella's presence. Otherwise, Tony might be a bloodied mess, left to rot back down on the trail. But he hadn't wanted her to think he was some kind of untrained hooligan. Then again, who was he kidding? He'd often solved his problems with his fists in the past, even though he knew there was a better way.

They stopped for a quick lunch of crackers and cheese. Wyatt didn't have the time or the energy to light a fire and cook up one of the dehydrated meals. He was more worried about trying to decide whether they should keep going. Should he change direction? Abandon their plan? There were lots of other trails up here. Technically, the hiking trails weren't open in winter, but the odd cross-country-skiing group still used them. They didn't have sufficient supplies to stay out here for more than another day or two, however. He'd need to restock if they were to keep traveling.

If someone had managed to pick up Tony's signal, would they even bother to follow them this far into the wilderness? Wyatt doubted it. Few people beside him were brave enough or stupid enough to go hiking in this weather.

Suddenly, he heard Stella's breaths coming in loud, ragged gasps, and he glanced behind him. He was a dick. She must be exhausted; they'd been climbing for over an hour without a break. He'd been worrying over other things and not concentrating on her. She hadn't complained, not even once. They were nearly to the summit of Butte Cabin Ridge. There was a perfect little campsite just over the other side, but they were still an hour's walk away.

"How are you doing? Can you make it for another few minutes? We'll be at the top then, and we should get an excellent view." He stopped and waited until Stella looked up at him.

Stella merely nodded, then returned her gaze to the trail, making sure she didn't stumble or fall. Tony had dropped back; he was barely visible through the trees. Wyatt couldn't be bothered waiting for him. He was thoroughly regretting bringing the man along. If he couldn't keep up, it was his own fault.

Wyatt listened to Stella struggle the rest of the way, grunting and gasping for air, and felt like a complete ass that he'd been ignoring her for so long.

But when they crested the top of the last rise and Stella stopped to take in the scenery, he knew the climb had been worth it. A few taller trees blocked their direct view into the next valley, but from here they could see the Bitterroot Mountains spread out on the other side of the basin.

"Wow," she breathed. "This is... I can't find the words. It's *trés magnifique*."

Wyatt didn't speak French, but even he could translate that. He straightened his shoulders, somehow absurdly glad she liked what she saw. Although, after her reaction when they escaped from the snowbound truck and she'd seen the spectacle left behind by the blizzard, calling it a winter wonderland, he should've known.

"I no longer mind that my legs are aching." She flashed him one of her gorgeous grins. Stella had removed her knit cap and gloves and opened her coat, probably sweating from the steep climb, even in this freezing weather. Her hair, which was normally swept up into a messy bun, had come loose and strands were hanging around her face, which was flushed pink with exertion. She pursed her rosebud lips as her gaze roamed over the all-encompassing vista. She was the picture of vitality and feminine strength. And he suddenly wanted her with all his heart. If she were in his life, he might become that better man he knew was hiding deep inside him somewhere. He would do it for her. Because she deserved it. He took a step toward her, gaze fixed on her lips, lost in the idea of her. His body hummed with need, and all he wanted was to kiss that perfect mouth.

"Holy shit, are you trying to kill me?" Tony broke his small moment of introspection with his crass comment.

Wyatt stepped away from Stella, as if being released from a dream.

"Who wants some water?" Wyatt held out a bottle of melted snow toward Stella, passing it to her just before Tony tried to snatch it away, and sent him a look that said, mind your manners.

As he watched Stella put the bottle to her lips and tip her head back to gulp the water, something flashed in the corner of his eye below them; down the way they'd come. Turning his head, he concentrated on the area, not bothering to listen to Tony, who was now droning on about how he would never climb another mountain in his life.

What was that? Had he imagined it? Just the sunlight glinting off the snow? Or the flash of a bird's wing as it darted from one tree to the next? He stared for a long time, but saw nothing more.

It was time to get moving, otherwise they wouldn't make it to the campsite before dark.

"Only about half an hour to go, then we can set up camp. Tomorrow's walk is all downhill."

"Yay," Stella cheered.

"Thank Christ," muttered Tony.

Wyatt smiled grimly to himself. Little did they know that walking downhill could be nearly as bad as going up.

Sooner than he hoped, the trail leveled off, and they emerged onto a small plateau. Wyatt was glad he spent his time exploring both mountain ranges around Stevensville. This was part of the Sapphire Ranges, which weren't as high as their cousins, the Bitterroots, across the valley. Which was probably a good thing for Stella and Tony. At the time, it'd been his version of an escape, fulfilling his desire to be alone. It'd been such an amazing thing to walk free and unencumbered after the confines of being locked in prison for two years. It was his form of healing. Thankfully, Levi and Cat seemed to understand his need to be outdoors and had let him be. He knew that a little way off the path was a natural clearing that'd be a perfect place to spend the night. Other hikers might've used this spot in spring and summer, but there'd be no one out here in these conditions. They hadn't passed a single soul in the entire time they'd walked so far.

There was enough light left to set up the tent and get the fire going. They might even get a beautiful sunset, with a clear sky, only a few wispy clouds on the horizon. Wyatt briefly tossed up whether he should light a fire. If someone was following them, it'd act like a signal in the night. But he knew Tony would never put up with sleeping in the cold and dark. So, he cleared a space in the snow and even found some rocks to mark out a small fire pit.

"I'll get some wood," Stella said, marching off into the

forest. He was impressed that he hadn't even had to ask her. She was getting the hang of this. Tony, on the other hand... Wyatt rolled his eyes in the man's direction. He'd dropped his backpack on the ground and sat down on the nearest log, resting his elbows on his knees, looking defeated and exhausted. Wyatt struggled to find an ounce of sympathy.

But then, as he watched Tony sitting like a rag doll, staring vacantly into the middle of the clearing, the man's bedraggled condition finally tugged at his emotions. His face was looking a lot worse for wear, and Wyatt flinched away, knowing he'd inflicted that damage with his own hands. Tonight, he'd show him how to make a bower of pine branches and needles to keep him off the freezing ground.

Stella came back and dropped an armload of dead wood next to his ring of stones. "Can you show me how to put the tent up tonight, please? I want to learn how to do these things."

"You bet," he said. "Give me a few minutes to light the fire."

She nodded and took out the bottle, draining the last of the water. Then she asked Wyatt for a pan and filled it with fresh snow, ready to melt for the trek tomorrow. He really should stop being so surprised by this woman and her tenacity. She was amazing. Maybe that was why he liked her so much.

They had dehydrated beef stew for dinner, which tasted like old leather, but at least it was hot and filled them up. Wyatt found a dead log and dragged it closer to the fire. He and Stella sat close together, their knees touching, staring into the flames. Tony had rolled himself up in his sleeping bag on his makeshift bed to stay warm. Pity they hadn't thought to bring a bottle of rum with them. It might've been nice sitting around the fire, drinking and talking. Almost as if they were on a normal camping trip.

"Will we reach the ruined house tomorrow? The place you

hid Tony's diamonds?" Stella asked.

Levi poked the fire with the stick, sending a shower of sparks up through the pine branches. At the mention of his name, Tony rolled over and cracked an eye open, but said nothing.

"Yes, it's at the base of this mountain, less than a day's walk. I'll call Levi in the morning and we can meet him there. He can give us any updates, bring us more supplies, and we can make a decision as to our next course of action."

"That sounds good." Stella nodded, but then hesitated. "Do you think there's any chance we might get to go home? That this might all be over?"

His heart broke at the careful hope he heard her voice. He knew from experience this was probably far from over. Dmytro would not let it be. They'd have to come up with some plan to give him back the diamonds and discover if there were any terms Dmytro might want to negotiate on. Dmytro's ruthlessness was renowned; he left no one he considered a traitor alive.

None of this showed on his face as he replied, "Maybe, we'll have to wait and talk to Levi."

"Talking about this man Dmytro, I'd like to know more about your life in prison, if you'll tell me. How did you get... get to know him?"

He guessed what she was really wondering was why he'd gotten involved with people like Tony and Dmytro? Where had his life gone so wrong? She had a right to know, seeing as how she was mixed in so deep with all this shit.

She went on before he could frame an appropriate answer. "I know you're innocent. But how did they get it so wrong?" Her green eyes glowed emerald in the light of the fire, filled with compassion and sensitivity. "Do you mind me asking?"

"I don't mind," he said, which wasn't the complete truth, because he hadn't spoken of it since he'd walked through those prison doors to freedom. He'd never mentioned it again; outside of his lawyers and the jury, no one knew the full story. But it was time. And maybe, just maybe, Stella might understand. Understand why he'd needed to befriend people like Tony, just to make it through.

Tony's eyes were closed. He may have been asleep or was possibly still listening to them. Either way, it didn't bother Wyatt.

"Zoe used to live next door to me. It was in one of those housing blocks, in the outer suburbs of Missoula. I wasn't always home, because I still liked to camp under the stars whenever I could. The walls are so thin in those apartments." He poked the stick into the flames again, his mind shifting gears as the painful memories came back. "But when I was home, I could hear what was going on next door. Zoe's husband, Tyrone, would regularly come home drunk and beat the crap out of her."

Wyatt tensed his fists on his knees. The noises coming from next door were often what drove him out into the wilds. It was probably going on in more than one apartment in the block, and Wyatt tried to tell himself it was none of his business. Tyrone was an enormous ball of muscle, a bodybuilder and a boxer, and so, while Wyatt had contemplated more than once going over and knocking on the door, telling him to quit it, he knew the outcome wouldn't be good. Even though he'd never confronted Tyrone, he'd done what he could. He befriended Zoe, hoping to make her life easier in some way.

Stella made a small noise of dismay, but said nothing, just let him continue.

"I got acquainted with Zoe, tried to look after her, you know? We'd drink coffee in the morning together. And sometimes shared a beer in the afternoon, and I would attempt to talk her into leaving that bastard. We got to know each other well."

Here came the part Wyatt wasn't proud of. Should he tell Stella? He swallowed hard, gritting his teeth to get the words out.

"We started...sleeping together." That was one way to put it, and probably mostly correct. He hadn't been in love with Zoe, he knew that now. But he'd felt sorry for her and when she came onto him, he hadn't had the courage to say no. He kept his gaze fixed on the flames, unwilling to meet Stella's eyes, afraid of what he might see there.

"I was trying to convince her to leave Tyrone, but she was so scared. Then she got pregnant. She told me it was mine, and I believed her."

Stella's hand snaked onto his knee, resting quietly there. It was a small offer of comfort, but it meant the world to him.

He could've made a life with Zoe. They talked about getting a new place, far away from there. They could move in together, have the baby, and he'd find a better job. She would divorce that bastard Tyrone, and he'd finally leave her alone. The fantasy had been real for him for a while, and that's when he'd convinced himself they were in love.

"I found us a new apartment to rent. She was going to leave him, to be with me." In his mind, they were going to make it. "Then she lost the baby."

That'd been devastating. Wyatt couldn't understand how he could feel a connection to something that didn't even exist yet. Zoe had been less than three months pregnant, the fetus merely the size of a walnut. But he felt the loss like a stake to the heart.

"Oh, no, Wyatt, I'm so sorry." Stella's hand tightened on his knee.

"The crazy thing was, Zoe went back to Tyrone after the miscarriage. He begged her to come home, said he'd stop beating her, get some help. I couldn't convince her we could still be together."

Why did some women do that? He shook his head in disbelief. Someone had told him later that she may have suffered from battered woman syndrome, which somehow made her feel like she caused the abuse; that if she could be a better wife, then he'd be a better husband.

"I decided to keep the new apartment, but on my last night in the old place, after I'd moved most of my stuff out, I heard Tyrone at it again. This time Zoe was really screaming, and so I went around and knocked on the door. Right before I got there, I heard her screaming cut off. I rushed in, and Tyrone was standing over her. He'd stabbed her through the heart and was still holding the knife. Stupidly, I knelt down to see if Zoe was okay and he knocked me out."

Stella gave a small gasp, but her gaze remained fixed on his face.

"He framed me, said that I was her scorned lover, and when she lost my baby and had gone back to him, I couldn't stand it, and killed her in a lover's rage."

"No!" Stella covered her mouth with both hands and her wide eyes filled with tears.

"I woke up being handcuffed by the police. Tyrone had fixed everything, he put my fingerprints on the knife, and the police found witnesses who said Zoe and I were having an affair."

It was the worst kind of betrayal. Wyatt had only been trying to help Zoe, and instead he'd ruined everything. She lost her life, and he'd lost his freedom. If only he'd left things alone, perhaps she'd still be alive. And he would be… What? He'd never have gone to jail, but then again, would he have been able to live with himself if he'd done nothing?

"The cops built a case against me and they sentenced me to twenty years."

"So, what happened? How did they catch Tyrone?" Her

hands still up at her face, Stella spoke through her fingers.

"An undercover cop, working on another case, chanced to overhear Tyrone telling a guy in a bar about how he got away with murder. The cop followed it up, and they arrested Tyrone a couple of months later."

"And then you were set free?" she asked.

"Yes, I was."

It sounded so simple. If only it were that easy. He'd never received one apology from any of the police who arrested him, or the lawyer who'd prosecuted him, or the judge who put him away. The justice system was broken, and it'd broken a small part of him, as well. Life since he'd left jail had been a rollercoaster of emotions. Being able to stay with Levi had been godsend, and finding the job at CJ's had also helped. But Wyatt knew he'd lost most of his self-esteem; he didn't know who he was anymore. Perhaps that was the main reason he'd agreed to hide Tony's package. Because he still had a strong connection to his life behind bars, couldn't quite disconnect himself from the people there and the obligations he felt to them.

"I'm sorry you had to go through all that," Stella whispered.

"So am I. But what's done is done."

"Thank you for telling me the truth."

He tried to mine her words for their true meaning. How did she really feel about him getting another man's wife pregnant and then trying to run away with her?

She turned toward him on the log and took off her gloves, then put a hand on either side of his face.

"I can't begin to understand what you must've been through. But I want you to know, I don't think any less of you." Her lips lightly brushed his, holding at the corner of his mouth, keeping him on the edge of temptation.

At least, now he had his answer.

"You're so different to any other man I've ever known," she whispered against his cheek. "But I like that. And I want to find out more. Know you more. Better."

His breath caught in his throat and something in his chest squeezed agonizingly. Was she saying what he thought she was saying?

He glanced at Tony. The man was snoring quietly.

Stella pulled his face back, her eyes darkening with desire in the firelight. This time when she kissed him, she left nothing to his imagination, her mouth closing over his, hot and demanding. The small sigh that escaped her throat had him going impossibly hard.

"The tent," she panted. "We need to go to the tent." She pulled him up by the hand and he followed willingly. He should stoke the fire. And he'd meant to patrol the perimeter of the camp before he went to sleep. But all that evaporated in his need to feel Stella in his arms.

CHAPTER THIRTEEN

Inside, the tent was lit with a soft haze from the glow of firelight. Stella was already reaching for Wyatt's coat buttons. She wanted to feel his skin beneath her hands. Wanted to delve in and explore those chiseled abs she knew were under his shirt.

"Wait a second." Wyatt did something with the two sleeping bags, and she gave an impatient whimper. "They zip together," he said, by way of explanation. Ooh, she liked these clever bags.

Then his obsidian eyes were on her, and he beckoned her to join him in the tangle of bedding. Quickly shedding her coat and hat, she climbed in beside him. It was too cold to get completely naked, but as he tugged her on top of his chest, she felt his hardened body beneath her and she trembled, imagining the different ways she could explore that same body. Her exploration would have to wait for another time, hampered as they were by all their layers. But she could still make this interesting. This was the most alive she'd felt in a long time. It'd started the moment Wyatt had rescued her from her crashed truck. It was Wyatt; he made her feel alive.

She was aware of his cock straining against the softness of her abdomen. She lowered her head and kissed him, her fingers busy lifting his hoodie and the hem of his shirt so she could finally skim her hands over all those steely muscles of his stomach beneath. Burying her nose against his neck, she drew in the smell of Wyatt

With a grunt, he flipped her over, and she lay on her back as he lingered above. He liked to be on top, it seemed. Maybe a little dominant. She liked it. She might also surprise him, because she liked to be on top, too. Her legs went loose, a liquid heat pooling in her belly at the thought. Her hands went to work, unzipping his jeans and helping him drag them down past his knees. It wasn't easy within the confines of the double sleeping bag, but she managed. Her fingers found the length of him and she stroked, easy and slow. Wyatt gave a soft curse, his mouth devouring hers. His nimble fingers encountered her waistband and soon her jeans and underwear joined his, stuffed down the bottom of the bags. Roaming underneath her shirt, his hands fumbled slightly, then released her bra and was kneading her breasts. She let out a sigh, only half remembering to stay quiet so as not to wake Tony.

She wrapped her legs around his hips. This was going to be quick and debauched and incredibly hot. Exactly what she needed right now.

"Wyatt."

He stopped kissing her to stare down with those dark, dark eyes unerringly focused on her.

"Have you got...?"

Something crinkled in his hand and she gave a purr of approval as he slipped the condom on. She loved a man who was prepared.

He hovered above her. "Are you sure?" His words were a vibration in her chest.

"Fais-moi l'amour, tout de suite."

Wyatt didn't seem to need a translation, he sank into her in one, slow, sensuous stroke.

* * *

Stella opened her eyes with a start. It was pitch black. Someone was whispering in her ear, urging her to wake up. Panic sank its claws into her belly, and she sat up, backing away from the voice. But this wasn't her bed back at Stargazer. Was she dreaming? Her head brushed against something soft and she let out a small scream. A hand came up to cover her mouth, and she began to struggle.

"Stella, it's me. You need to be quiet."

It was Wyatt. The sound of his voice kick-started her brain, and she suddenly remembered where she was, the disorientation clearing. Of course, she was in a tent, and they were on a mountainside. What was going on? Why had he woken her up like this? Like a thief in the night.

Especially after what they'd shared. Had she and Wyatt really made love earlier? She didn't regret it one bit.

"Do you promise to be silent?" he whispered in her ear. She nodded, and he slowly removed his hand from her mouth. "We need to get out of here. Right now. Leave everything behind."

So many questions circled her mind, but the urgency in his voice had icicles running down her spine. Something was terribly wrong. Glad that'd she'd re-dressed after their tryst—it was too cold to sleep otherwise—she grabbed her coat and felt in the pockets for her gloves and hat.

Stella emerged from the tent, following close on Wyatt's heels. Her heart beat wildly in her chest. The fire had died right down, with only smoldering coals remaining. Which meant it was some hours since they'd crawled into the tent together. Outside the ring of firelight, Stella could see nothing but inky blackness. Wyatt moved swiftly around the fire, picking up Tony's backpack as he went. Tony's sleeping bag was spooled on top of his bed of branches, but the man was nowhere to be seen. She was about to ask where he'd gone, but Wyatt put a finger to his lips and then handed her the backpack soundlessly. Wyatt was already shouldering into his own pack, so Stella slung Tony's on.

Where was Tony? Had he run away in the night? Betrayed them? But why would he do that? He'd end up lost and probably die alone on the mountainside. Even he wasn't that stupid. And he certainly wouldn't have left his backpack behind. Had he turned against them for some reason? Was it him they were fleeing?

Suddenly, it hit her. The only scenario she could think of that would make Wyatt act like this was if someone had found them. Tracked them through the wilderness. The knot of fear in her belly tightened into something almost alive as it climbed its way up her throat. This was the stuff of nightmares.

"Hold on to the back of my bag, so you don't get lost in the dark," he whispered into her ear. "No flashlights," he warned.

She did as she was told, and soon, they melted into the darkness of the surrounding forest. Her legs were wobbly with adrenaline as she tried to keep her ragged breathing under control, but she maintained her death grip on Wyatt's bag. A couple of times, Wyatt stopped, and they stood in the silence, listening. When he was satisfied he heard nothing, they went on. All she could hear was the rapid thumping of her heartbeat in her ears.

They were heading to the right of their camp, going slightly downhill. Even in the pitch dark, Wyatt was taking great pains to place his feet carefully. Stella understood he was trying not to displace the snow, making sure each footfall was securely placed. It felt like they were traveling at a snail's pace and the blood hammering thorough Stella's veins was urging her to go faster. But Wyatt must have a reason for his stealth, so she took a couple of deep breaths and tried to copy his movements as best she could. The weight of Tony's backpack hampered her, but she didn't complain.

Slowly, her eyes adjusted to the dark, like they had the night before last, on the forced march away from Levi's house. Enough starlight filtered through the pine needles for her to make out the denser shapes of tree trunks, as well as be able to avoid getting smacked in the face by low-hanging branches. The moon would rise at some stage. Last night, it'd peaked over the ridgeline just as she was crawling into her tent. Right now, she had no idea of the time. It could be nine o'clock, or it could be well after midnight, for all she knew.

An image of her mother's disapproving face appeared in Stella's mind. What would she think if she saw her daughter now? Probably the first words out of her mouth would be, *I told you so.* And for once, she might be right. For once, Stella wished she'd heeded her mother's words, and she could be safely tucked up in her bed in the apartment in Lyon, instead of fleeing a band of killers in the middle of the night. Stella almost wished for Armand's steadying presence. But then she remembered, he'd most likely frown and look down his nose at her, using that disparaging tone to tell her she should stick to what she knew.

She was much better off with Wyatt's strong, quiet leadership.

They kept going, slowly but surely, for around half an hour, by Stella's reckoning. Finally, Wyatt came to a halt next to a fallen log. He listened for at least a minute, but then he peeled off his backpack and turned to help her do the same. Stella sat gratefully on the log. Her legs had been stiff and sore from their climb yesterday, and now they were weak and shaky. She felt a little lightheaded, and her mouth was as dry as a chip.

"We need to stay quiet," he whispered. "But I don't think

we've been followed." He rummaged around in a side pocket of his backpack, handing her a bottle of water. "This is our only one, be careful with it. I didn't have time to grab any more."

Stella wondered at his forethought even to pick up this one, which'd been sitting by the fire, the snow slowly melting inside.

"What's going on? Who's following us?" she whispered back, holding onto the bottle, but not drinking from it yet.

He sat beside her, but his head swiveled from side to side as he constantly checked their surroundings. She kept her ears primed, but could hear nothing, except the soft sigh of the wind rustling the branches higher up and a bird calling in a low, misery-filled voice. An owl, perhaps?

"I heard something, a noise. You were fast asleep. I wasn't sure what it was, so I got up to investigate. When I got outside, Tony's bed was empty."

Stella drew in a sharp breath, and he nodded in agreement. "I have to admit, I thought the worst of the little prick, too. I thought he might've abandoned us, not that would've been such a bad thing. I decided it was more likely he'd got up to take a leak."

"Then what?" Stella urged when he stopped talking and stared out through the tree trunks, as if contemplating some deep, inner notion.

"I heard the same noise again, the one that woke me in the first place, and followed the sound uphill, away from camp. I thought it might be a fox or a wolf hunting a rabbit, but I noticed some marks in the snow, like something had been dragged up the hill. Then I saw..." Wyatt hesitated, a catch in his voice.

Stella held her breath.

"Tony is dead," Wyatt said bluntly. "I saw him, his hands and feet were tied together. He was helpless, and the guy just..." Again, Wyatt stopped talking.

"What guy? Are you sure?" What did he mean, the guy? Was there just one of them? Stella wondered how much he'd been able to see in the dark. What if Tony were still alive? Should they go back for him?

"The guy had a big knife, and he slit his throat, like he was butchering a pig."

Stella covered her mouth to stop herself from crying out. Oh, no. What a terrible thing to happen. Even though she hadn't liked Tony, she didn't wish death on anyone. Especially not a violent, abhorrent death like this one.

"After I saw that, I didn't stay any longer. I hightailed it back to the camp to get you. I don't know if the other guy heard me, but Tony was making a horrible, gurgling noise, so maybe that covered the sound of my retreat."

Oh, God, Stella thought she might be sick. Her throat closed up, and she brought her hands to her mouth. This wasn't real; this couldn't be real.

Wyatt's head stopped its constant swiveling, and he turned his dark gaze towards her. "I'm so sorry, Stella. I'm sorry you had to hear that, and I'm sorry you have to go through all of this." He put a protective arm around her shoulders. She leaned against his solid chest, drawing in his strength.

"Do you think that guy was alone? Will he follow us?" She asked. Were they in danger too? If it was Dmytro's hitman they'd been talking about, then wasn't he only after Tony? Perhaps now, if he really had killed Tony, he'd leave them alone. Cold broke through the thick layer of her coat. She shivered, suddenly feeling frozen to the marrow of her bones.

"I only saw one man. I'm pretty sure he's alone," Wyatt assured her. "But whether he follows us, or not, well, that depends."

"On what?" Stella asked. Why was he being so cryptic?

Instead of answering her, he bent down and picked up

Tony's backpack. Unzipping a small, side pocket, he dug his fingers into the cavity. To her horror, he gripped a little black bag, and she gave a soft groan.

"It depends on whether or not he thinks we have the diamonds," Wyatt said.

CHAPTER FOURTEEN

Wyatt slipped the little black bag back into the compartment. "Come on, we need to get moving." He pulled Stella in for one last embrace, and then let her go. She'd been shivering almost uncontrollably, and he'd held her until her trembling had subsided. She hadn't cried, for which he was forever grateful. And again, he found himself surprised at her fortitude. She was handling this better than most women. Perhaps Cat might've been more capable, but she was the strongest woman he knew.

Images of their lovemaking flashed through his mind, but he pushed them away

Whoever this guy was that'd been tracking them, he seemed to have some skills when it came to surviving in the wilderness. And he was also clearly fit and strong to have caught up to them so quickly. They would've had at least half a day's head start, so this man had walked through the night and all today. Could it be the feared Anton Babich that Tony mentioned?

The only possible way he could've found them was when Tony checked his phone last night. There were numerous trails leading up this mountain, but there'd been no snowfall recently to cover their tracks. So, if this guy was a half-decent outdoorsman, he wouldn't have found it hard to follow their trail, once he picked it up. And when Tony studied his phone again at lunchtime today, that could've cemented in the hunter's mind that he was going in the right direction. If only Wyatt had listened to his instincts, chosen another path, or taken off across-country, they might have been able to avoid this killer.

Standing, he pulled Stella to her feet. The guy would find it hard to track them in the dark, but it wouldn't be impossible, and he was conceivably already on their trail. They'd have to move faster, and just hope they didn't make too much noise. The more distance they put between them and whoever was up there, the better.

"Are you all right to get going?" She didn't need to know everything he was thinking. Even though she was tough, she might crack under that sort of pressure. He had to keep them moving and continue to stay positive. They'd head for the ruined house. There was no way he was going to follow a path this time, however. It'd be hard work slogging through the virgin forest. It'd slow them down, but also make their trail harder to track. But not impossible; their prints would still be visible in the snow, even in the dark. He'd call Levi on the sat phone once it was light to see if they could come up with another plan.

Helping Stella shrug on Tony's backpack, he slipped his on, as well, then led them downhill. He'd tossed around the idea of carrying both backpacks to save Stella from having to do it, but knew that'd put him at a severe disadvantage if it came to having to run, or fight for their lives. They walked in silence for the next half an hour, both lost in their own thoughts.

A part of Wyatt wondered if the guy who'd killed Tony would have allowed them their freedom if he'd found the diamonds. Should he have left the bag for the hitman to find?

Deep down, Wyatt already knew the answer. And at least now, they had a bargaining chip, something to use to negotiate with Dmytro.

Stella seemed to know what he was thinking, because she finally broke the silence by asking, "Can't we just get rid of them? Throw them away? If we don't have diamonds, then surely that's the end, isn't it?"

"That would be the simple solution," he replied. A part of him liked that Stella had no compunction to keep the diamonds. At least he knew for certain she wasn't driven by greed. He wondered idly how much the gems were worth. How much would Tony have been willing to risk his life for? Everyone had a price, but Wyatt had no idea how much Tony would sell his soul for. He suspected it'd have to be in the hundreds of thousands.

"But it's never that simple," he continued. "If we told Dmytro we threw them away, he wouldn't believe us, even if it was the truth. People like that can't see that people like us aren't driven by greed. He'd hunt us down, and we'd never be safe."

There was a brief silence as Stella digested his words. He pushed aside a low-hanging branch and held it while Stella went through. Wyatt glanced over his shoulder, something he'd been doing every few minutes since they left the log.

There was a flicker of light up above them on the mountainside.

"Shh," he said urgently, grabbing Stella by the arm.

"Wha—?" He put a finger to her lips and pulled her behind a large tree trunk.

They waited for what seemed an eternity. Just when Wyatt thought he'd imagined it, there it was again. A definite shimmer, like someone using a flashlight. It went off as quickly as it'd gone on. The guy was probably checking he was on the right trail, making sure he didn't miss the footprints. Wyatt cursed the snow. If it'd been any other time of year, it would've been almost impossible to track them through the dense, dark forest. But it was as if they'd left a glaring neon sign behind, pointing in their direction.

Stella gave a frightened squeak of alarm when the flashlight had flared. But now she was unbearably silent, staring up at the patch of forest where the killer was stalking them. Levi couldn't hear anything, which meant this guy was clearly intelligent and well versed in outdoorsmanship, if he could descend so quickly and quietly behind them.

What were they going to do?

They could make a dash for it, straight down the mountain, not caring how much noise they made and try to outrun the guy.

But where would they run to? They were miles away from any roads or houses. How would Stella cope? She was already exhausted from their hike up to the summit yesterday. And now, running on very little sleep and a whole heap of adrenaline, he might be asking too much of her. The man would surely catch them before they made it halfway to safety.

He'd been too blasé, thinking this guy wouldn't intercept them. Again, it was another mistake he'd made, and now he'd put Stella in even more danger. If he'd been on his own, he might've been able to outfox this hitman.

It'd been a mistake to make love to Stella tonight; to let himself fall under her spell. If only he'd checked the perimeter, like he wanted to, then maybe… But no, he could never think of making love with Stella as a mistake. He would give it all up again for another night with her.

But right now, he had no other option.

He was going to have to stand and fight.

Stella would not like this, but he prayed she followed his instructions. Dumping his backpack on the ground near

Stella's feet, he dug into the depths until he found what he was looking for. The large hunting knife in the leather sheath that he'd made by hand himself. He tucked the blade inside the breast of his coat.

Levi's gun was a heavy weight in his pocket.

"I need you to wait here for me," he whispered.

Her face was a pale oval in the starlight as she turned to look at him. "What? You're not leaving me? You can't—"

He placed a finger over her lips. Handing her the pistol, he asked, "Have you ever used one of these?"

"No, of course not." Her whisper was getting louder by the second. They were running out of time; the guy probably had a bead on them already. Wyatt was hoping the man's chief aim was the diamonds. If that were true, he wouldn't kill them until he knew where they were. It was a gamble, but one Wyatt was prepared to take.

"I don't have time to argue. If this guy gets past me, you're going to have to use this to save yourself. Okay?" In any other instance, Wyatt would take the gun himself, but that would leave Stella completely unprotected and he wasn't inclined to do that. He was skilled at using a knife, had killed many wild animals with one when he'd been hunting for food.

"I don't..." the rest of her words faded out to a low whimper. Wyatt steeled his emotions. He couldn't let Stella's nervousness override what he had to do.

"It's easy." Taking her hand in his, he moulded her palm against the butt of the pistol and put her finger on the trigger. "I've already unlocked the safety catch. All you have to do is point and fire. It has ten bullets. If you need to use it, make sure each one counts Make sure he's close enough that you can't miss."

"*Merde*," she whispered.

"I'm hoping you won't have to use this," he said, running a

finger down her cheek. "I'm going to sneak up behind him, try to capture him."

A twig snapped not far away, and both of them looked up. The guy had gotten careless. Wyatt had wasted precious time trying to convince Stella. But this might play into their hands, because now there was no doubt the man knew where they were and was heading straight for them. In a way, he was going to use Stella as bait, draw the killer towards her, while he snuck around behind him.

Stella was still staring at him, the gun held away from her body at an awkward angle. He didn't want to leave her. She'd be alone; a target in the night. He leaned in and kissed her on the lips. If it was the last time he ever got to see her, at least he had that.

"I'll see you soon," he promised.

Gliding noiselessly around the side of the large trunk, Wyatt headed off at a tangent, away from where the man was descending above them. He used every skill he'd ever learned to creep his way up the mountainside. Silent and deadly, he slipped into hunter mode—stalking his prey. He was doing this to protect Stella, he kept reminding himself. To protect the other people he loved. Protect Levi and Cat.

There was a tiny part of him that also wanted to avenge Tony's death. Even though Tony had got him into this whole mess, and even though Tony would most likely have ended up back in jail, no one deserved to die that way.

It took him less than a minute to circle around, pushing stealthily through the bushes. He would've liked to take a wider arc, bringing him around so he came down from above, giving him the advantage of higher ground. But he couldn't take the chance this man would get too close to Stella. So, instead, he came in at an angle, almost parallel with the slope of the mountain.

Wyatt glimpsed the man through the trees, a dark shape

moving against the black background. He stopped and watched for a few seconds, making sure he didn't know Wyatt was there. The bulge on the other man's back hinted he was carrying a small backpack. Was that a rifle slung over his shoulder? He heard that Babich used a rifle as his weapon of choice. Shit. Wyatt's guts quivered at the thought of going up against such a man. It meant Anton was armed not only with the knife he'd killed Tony with, but a gun, as well. He'd have to make sure he got in nice and close, so Anton wouldn't have time to use the rifle. If it came down to a knife fight, the odds might be more on Wyatt's side.

Closer and closer, Wyatt crept, stalking Anton. The other man's focus was mostly downhill, towards the spot where Stella was hiding. But this man was no rookie, and he was also aware of his surroundings, twisting his head to check behind, and stopping to listen every few paces.

Wyatt got to within ten feet, when the man turned and stared in his direction. Wyatt was exposed, stalking between one tree trunk and the next. Anton spotted him. He raised his rifle.

Wyatt charged, yelling loudly. He had no clear intention of killing the man. All he wanted to do was stop him. He hit the man with the full force of his body, sending him flying backwards, just as the gun went off. The bullet went wide, Wyatt knocking the weapon out of his grip as he landed on top of him.

The knife was in Wyatt's hand and he stabbed down with all his force; heard a grunt as the blade bit into flesh. The man was reaching for his ankle, probably had his knife in a holster around his leg. Wyatt had to stop him from getting that knife, or he was a dead man.

The man was powerful, taller than Wyatt, and wiry like a greyhound. They wrestled. Anton got an arm around Wyatt's neck and dragged him sideways, using his legs to try to turn them over, so Wyatt was beneath him. He couldn't let that happen, his knife hand was free and so he stabbed repeatedly at the man's shoulders, catching him with a glancing blow. But it was enough to make Anton cry out and release him, defending himself from the blows.

Snow was flying everywhere; there was snow in Wyatt's mouth and eyes, blinding him. The man was holding a hand to his shoulder to staunch the flow of blood, and he stopped struggling. Was he giving up? Wyatt drew in a huge gulp of air. Was this it? Had he won?

Sensing Wyatt's hesitation, the man let out a bloodcurdling yell and shoved Wyatt with all his might, knocking him onto his back in the snow. Wyatt saw him reaching for the knife at his ankle, saw the flash of a blade in the light of the stars, and then Anton was standing over him.

"You little punk. I might've left you alive. But not anymore. I'll get what I need from your girlfriend, and then I'll kill her, too." It was too dark to see the man's facial features, but his voice was deep and terrifying in the still night air.

Stella, he had to protect Stella. Rolling sharply to the right, Wyatt used the slope of the hill to get his feet under him and then he was standing, facing Anton. They circled each other like two wary mountain lions, each with a knife in their hand. Wyatt was panting hard, out of breath, adrenaline pumping through his veins, making him twitchy and unstable.

Wyatt held the lower ground. Not good. Anton was taller than him, and now he had the advantage of being uphill. He waited, his sparring experience in prison standing him in good stead, making sure he didn't dive in first. Let Anton come to him. He used those few precious seconds to try to get his breath back.

But it seemed Anton was doing the same thing, because he asked, "Tell me where the diamonds are, and I'll leave you alone." Wyatt didn't believe him for a second. Was the other man just buying time? He couldn't see how bad the wounds he'd inflicted were in the dark. He'd got Anton at least twice, but without being able to gauge the blood flow, he had no idea if they were merely flesh wounds, or something more serious.

The man opened his mouth as if to say something further, and Wyatt took the opportunity. He feinted right, then swung the knife across to his left hand and lunged low toward the man's legs, slicing across his shin bone. The maneuver landed him on his belly on the ground, and he quickly rolled onto his back.

Anton let out an anguished yell and clutched at his leg, while sweeping his blade down toward Wyatt's face. It was sheer instinct that saved Wyatt, blocking the blade with his own knife. But he felt the swish of air, as the metal passed so close to his cheek he could have called it a shave. Anton's enraged thrust put him off balance, and now he teetered on one leg, before crashing down onto the snow-sodden earth beside Wyatt. Without thinking, Wyatt rolled and then levered himself up, jumping onto Anton's prone body and driving the knife down into the man's unprotected neck.

Anton made a strangled gurgle, and both hands flew to his throat. Even in the dim light, Wyatt could see his eyes opened wide in surprise, reflecting the starlight in their depths.

He kicked out weakly, still grasping at his neck, trying to speak. But only feeble gurgles left his lips.

Wyatt watched as the light slowly left the other man's eyes.

There was a sound, like the sighing of the wind high in the branches. But this sound came from the man lying on the snow beneath him.

Anton went limp, eyes open and staring at the sky.

He was dead.

Anton's last wild swing at Wyatt's face had been an

amateurish blow, ferocious and unthinking, and it made Wyatt wonder if the man had actually been suffering from blood loss, or pain from his wounds, or both, to become impaired like that. It might explain why he'd been able to beat Anton—who seemed to have been well-trained in the art of fighting. Whatever the reason, Anton was dead. And Wyatt was alive.

He'd killed a man.

The words echoed around his brain.

While he'd been in prison, he'd become good at using his hands to defend himself. He'd beaten other men to a bloody pulp, but never before had he taken a life. Behind those bars, he'd seen other men knifed in the stomach, sliced across the chest, one even had his eye gouged out. He'd seen other inmates using handmade shivs to wound and maim. Wyatt never used one himself, even though he knew how to handle a knife, had become proficient with one living off the land. Killing an animal, slitting its throat, was completely different to killing a man, however. His guts were quivering like a plate of jelly, and his knees could no longer hold his weight as he sank to the ground.

Was he going back to jail for murder? He couldn't do that. If he had to go back to prison, it would surely kill him.

CHAPTER FIFTEEN

"Stop right there." Stella made her voice sound loud and commanding, even though her hands were shaking so much she didn't think she'd be able to pull the trigger.

She'd stayed where Wyatt had told her, crouching behind the tree, staring into the dark, willing her eyes to see through the blackness. The sounds of men fighting on the slope above her were intense and horrifying. Stella had no idea what was going on or who was winning. Every now and then she caught the flash of something in the night, part of a dark shape moving between the trees.

The gun was an alien, cold thing in the palm of her hand. She prayed, and she watched and waited.

Then the clamor of the fighting stopped as abruptly as it started. Everything went deathly silent. She wanted to call out, to ask if Wyatt was okay, but dared not, in case the other man had won the battle. Was he out there right now, stalking through the underbrush, coming to get her?

A noise like that of a stealthy footfall alerted her. Was someone moving down the slope? She took a chance and peered around the side of the tree trunk. A dark shape slipped between two fir trees. Was it Wyatt? Or the hitman? She had no way of knowing. Crouching down again, she hunkered against the bark, willing the man to go away. Willing this all to go away. She didn't know what to do.

There was another sound, closer now. Whoever it was, they were coming straight toward her. If it was Wyatt, why hadn't he called out? It must be the other man. The one who'd butchered Tony. She began to tremble. Had he killed Wyatt? He'd left her his gun. She should've forced him to take it; to protect himself. And now he was dead because of her.

But he'd given her his weapon for this exact reason. She looked down and saw the hard metal shape in her hand. Lifting her head, she made a decision. She could do this. Do it for Wyatt. Her palm closed around the pistol, her finger finding the trigger like Wyatt had shown her. Just as the unmistakable sound of a boot crunching through the snow reached her, she got to her feet, holding the gun with both hands like she'd seen people do on the television.

Sucking in a giant breath, she rounded the edge of the trunk, pointing the gun at the shape emerging out of the dark. "Stop right there," she commanded.

"Stella, it's me." The sound of Wyatt's voice was sweet music to her ears.

"Oh, thank the Lord." She lowered the pistol and placed it carefully on the ground next to her, wanting to be rid of it. "You scared me. I didn't know if it was you or…"

He was there in front of her, solid and sure and alive. His muscular arms embraced her, pulling her in and holding her tight. She began to shake all over again, this time with relief, as the adrenaline left her body.

"It's okay, I'm here now. Everything's going to be okay," he soothed, stroking her hair, and murmuring to her like she was a lost child. They stayed like that for many minutes, her clinging to him and him grasping her tight, just breathing.

At last, she drew back, because she needed the answer.

"What happened? Is he…?" She couldn't say the word.

"I took care of him. We're safe. He won't bother us again," Wyatt replied, also backing away from her. "I might sit down for a second, if that's okay." He sat down heavily, his face as pale as the surrounding snow. She sat next to him, both of them unable to articulate what they were feeling.

So, the man was dead. Wyatt didn't need to say it. He'd killed someone. To protect her. And to protect himself. She wasn't sure how she felt about that. At the moment, it was sheer relief they were safe. She didn't really want to think about the man's corpse lying up there on the slope. Her mind was numb with fear and shock; she'd have to process it later. One thing she knew, Wyatt's silence spoke volumes. He was completely shocked by what he'd done.

He turned to face her. "I'm proud of you. You stood up to me as if I were the stranger, like I told you to."

"I'm not sure I could have pulled the trigger," she admitted.

"I think maybe you could."

She mulled over his comment, unconvinced if he was right.

He checked his watch. "Dawn is still an hour away." He hesitated, as if trying to come to a decision. "I'm going to call Levi on the sat phone. I don't care if he's asleep. We need help with this."

Ten minutes later, they were on the move again. Headed down the mountain toward the ruined house. Wyatt thought she might need to rest longer, but the idea of a dead body lying somewhere nearby, along with the pre-dawn, intense cold, had made up her mind. Wyatt was worried about her physical and mental health. But she discovered she could lock the events of tonight away in a box in her mind, to be analyzed and perhaps freaked out over, later. It was good to have a plan; good to be moving again. It stopped her from thinking too much, kept her body warm and active.

"What else did Levi say?" she asked as they shouldered their packs. She'd waited impatiently as Wyatt spoke to his brother, but once she'd found out they were going ahead with their meeting, she decided they could walk and talk, Wyatt could fill her in with the rest of it on the way. A tiny part of her hoped that when they reached the old house, she'd be able to go home. This whole thing might've blown over by then. Especially with the hitman dead.

"Levi said he'd been awake for most of the night. He's worried, and I don't blame him. Things are getting messy in town. Everyone is on high alert. The townsfolk are on edge, and they've called in more cops from Missoula. The place is swarming with them. And most of them are looking for me."

"That's not good."

"No, it's not," he sighed. "But there's been no sign of the people we're worried about. Dmytro's thugs seem to have gone to ground."

Hope flared in Stella's chest. "Maybe there was only one man. Maybe Anton was alone on this mission." Then she remembered there'd been two men showing photos at CJ's "Or perhaps they've left. The cops might've scared them away." She wanted to say maybe they were safe, but that was tempting fate.

Wyatt shook his head, and the hope died. No, of course they hadn't left. That'd be too easy. Her shoulders sagged, Tony's bag suddenly feeling like a lead weight. The idea of being able to return to Stargazer Ranch as if nothing had happened quickly fading.

"Levi has been keeping a low profile, so far. But now he knows they followed us, and this threat is real, he's pressing to dig deeper. Put some pressure on his friend at the sheriff's office for some more information. He's going to ask Jude to talk to Dmytro."

"But he's in prison, isn't he?"

"Yes, up in Missoula. But Levi will tell Jude he thinks there's a connection between Bryce's murder and this mob boss. Perhaps, if they can shake him up a bit, he might pull his men out."

"Do you think that'll work?"

Stella could imagine the lift of Wyatt's eyebrows as he answered. "No. Dmytro doesn't scare that easily."

"So where does that leave us?"

"At the moment, Levi is going to bring us fresh supplies. We need another tent, and some food."

Stella tensed her shoulders, but she couldn't rid herself of her growing irritation. "How long do you think we're going to need to stay out in this wilderness?" The thought of spending another night out in the freezing cold—even if it was sleeping next to Wyatt—had a knot of despair rising in her stomach. She trusted Wyatt. This crazy situation had shown her how much she could depend on him. He was courageous and faithful. He'd do anything to protect her. And perhaps she might even be falling for him.

But she couldn't do this anymore.

"I know this isn't ideal, but it's the only way I can keep us safe." Wyatt said.

"What if we try to negotiate?" She'd asked this question before, but perhaps there was a way to persuade this mob boss they were no threat, hand the diamonds back, and be done with it.

Wyatt lifted his shoulders and kept on walking.

At the thought of the jewels, she stopped. That was the core of the matter. If they could solve the problem of what to do with them, then they could call this whole thing off.

She stared at Wyatt's back for a few seconds, then called out, "So, what *are* we going to do with the diamonds?"

He considered her words for a second. "I might have an idea..."

CHAPTER SIXTEEN

Wyatt was on his knees, peering through the cover of a large chokeberry shrub. That was definitely Levi's truck parked in the driveway. The ranger logo on the side of the mud-splattered door stood out clearly in the midday sun. So why did he feel uneasy? Why was the back of his neck prickling with a thousand needles?

He scanned the area again. And again, everything looked calm. Nothing moved. Nothing looked out of place.

"Are Cat and Levi waiting inside?" Stella whispered in his ear.

"I don't know, I guess so." He hadn't really discussed that part of the plan with Levi. Maybe that's what was making him uneasy. Perhaps he'd been expecting Levi to be standing at the front door, watching for him. But that'd be ridiculous, like waving a red flag to anybody watching. Much like leaving his highly identifiable truck parked out the front for anyone to see. And suddenly, Wyatt knew what was worrying him. Why had Levi done something so obvious?

He waited and watched for another five minutes, while Stella became more and more agitated beside him. But nothing moved, and there was no sign of danger. He even tried calling Levi on the sat phone, but there was no answer.

Perhaps he'd left it in his truck.

"Are we going?" Stella finally said. She wasn't happy with this morning's turn of events. When he'd said they may have to go back out into the mountains, she'd argued a little at first, but after he'd agreed to hide the diamonds, she seemed to recover most of her good spirits.

He took a deep breath. They couldn't wait here forever; the chill was eating into his bones while they sat unmoving. "Stay behind me," he said. They crossed the bare, snowy ground between their hiding place and the house as quickly and silently as they could. When they reached the back wall, he peered through the broken glass of a window. He well knew the layout of this house, after he'd the nights he'd spent camping here. This back room had probably been a bedroom at one stage. An old dresser, with its drawers hanging open, sat against one wall, and the remains of a metal bed frame crouched in the middle of the room. The roof had caved in and snow and leaves now littered the wooden floorboards. There was no trace of anyone having been in there; no footprints in the snow, nothing had been changed or touched.

The back entrance gaped open to their right, the door hanging off its hinges, left to swing open. Wyatt poked his head around the edge of the doorframe. It was a small mud room leading into a kitchen. Nothing moved inside. The roof remained intact here, and so it was harder to see if anything had disturbed the dust and the debris. He thought he could see footprints scuffing through the rubbish. Perhaps Levi had come to the back door to peer outside. For no particular reason, Wyatt reached into his pocket and drew out the pistol. He felt a little safer with it in his hand.

Checking to make sure Stella was close behind, he motioned for her to follow him through the door. They emerged into the kitchen. Everything looked untouched, just the way he'd left it last time he'd been here.

He was being silly. "Cat. Levi, are you here?" he called softly.

There was silence for a few seconds, and then a slight scuffling noise. "We're in here," his brother called from the living room.

Wyatt lowered the gun with a sigh of relief and rounded through the door, Stella close on his heels.

There was Levi, standing in the doorway opposite, with a strange look on his face. Where was Cat? The room was as full of dust and wreckage as the rest of the house. Two sagging wooden chairs sat together in the corner, as if they were having a quiet conversation. An old table rested on three legs, pushed against the far wall. Wyatt took a half-step toward his brother, a smile of greeting forming on his face. But his smile froze when Levi stumbled forward and an unfamiliar man appeared behind him, a gun pointed at Levi's head.

Wyatt brought up his own gun, making certain Stella was tucked safely behind him. He knew he wouldn't shoot, as the other guy was using Levi as a shield. He couldn't take the risk.

"I'm sorry, Wyatt. They hurt Cat." The anguish in Levi's voice tore a hole in Wyatt's chest.

"Shut up, fucker," the man holding Levi snarled.

There was a sound behind him, and Stella gasped. He swiveled his head just enough to make out another figure stepping through the kitchen door in his peripheral vision.

Fuck.

He must've snuck around the outside of the house to come up behind them. They were trapped. Why hadn't he listened to that foreboding feeling earlier?

"Nice to meet you, young Mr. Wilson," the man pointing a gun at Levi drawled in a southern accent. He was tall, with sandy hair and a mischievous smile. Not the sort of guy he would've chosen to be a strong-arm for a mob boss. "You've been leading us on quite a dance."

"Lower your weapon," the guy in the kitchen growled at Wyatt.

His little finger twitched, but otherwise Wyatt didn't move. What the fuck was he gonna do now? *Think, Wyatt, think.*

"I'd do as he suggests," the Southerner said. "He's not in the best of moods. You killed his friend. And I think he's got revenge on his mind. That's quite a feat, by the way. Killing Anton Babich. He had a big reputation. Never liked the man much myself, but I'm certain Dmytro will miss him. Now, he's going to have to train a brand-new hitman."

Stella squeaked in fear behind him and a third outline appeared in the doorway to their left, leading off to another hallway and bedrooms. The man was a black shadow looming in the gloom, but Wyatt saw enough to know he was also pointing a gun at them.

Three against one. Wyatt lowered his weapon. They outnumbered him. He reached around and pulled Stella farther behind him, shielding her with his body as best he could, using the wall to protect her, as well.

Anton's friend was dark and swarthy, stocky like a mountain goat. Wyatt knew from the rumors that Anton was from Chechnya. It was part of his scary reputation, then he'd lived through the war with Russia, suffered through terrible atrocities, the sight of which had turned him into a killing machine. This guy looked to be of the same origin.

"Hand over the gun," the man with the accent demanded. Wyatt laid it on the floor. The other fellow in the shadows came forward and picked it up, then went back to lean against the doorframe, tucking Wyatt's pistol into his coat pocket. He was short, barely came to Wyatt's shoulder, but had a wicked scar starting at his ear and running down his neck. Wyatt shuddered at the sight.

How did they know Anton was dead? Unless... Levi must've told them. He'd poured out the whole sordid story to Levi over the sat phone this morning. How had they captured Levi? His brother had said they were being careful; they'd stayed at Stargazer Ranch. Had these men somehow infiltrated the ranch? Or had they got to Levi another way? Whatever. It didn't really matter. They'd used Levi and Cat to get to him, and now he had to do something, or they were all going to die.

"I may as well get to the point. You know what we're here for. Hand them over." The Southerner waved his gun abstractly in the air.

Wyatt swallowed hard, letting his gaze slip between the Southerner and the Chechen.

"I don't have them. But if you let Stella and my brother go, I'll lead you to the diamonds."

"What do you mean, you don't have them?" The mischievous smile disappeared from the man's face. His handsome features transformed, going hard, his eyes flint-like. Wyatt could suddenly see this guy might be dangerous, after all.

"They're still up on the mountain, with Tony."

"You're lying," the Chechen snarled.

"No, I'm not. You can check our bags, you can even pat me down," Wyatt replied quickly. He shivered at the idea of either of those two running their hands over him, or God forbid, Stella, but he needed them to believe him. They honestly didn't have the diamonds on them.

"Like my friend here says, I don't believe you," the Southerner cut in. "You see, Anton phoned in a sit rep, right after he killed Tony. Said that the jewels were nowhere to be found, and he was going after you two."

"Well, he must not have looked very hard, because Tony never let those diamonds out of his sight. I'm telling you, we don't have them. Tony had them on him. Either that, or he hid them somewhere near the camp. Take a look, if you don't believe me." He began to slowly ease the backpack over his shoulder, motioning for Stella to do the same.

This situation had all gone to shit. Not only was Stella involved, but now Levi and Cat had been put in mortal danger. Wyatt's guts churned. Levi had said they harmed Cat. What had they done to her? He felt sick, his throat constricting with the urge to dry retch.

He was going to get them out of this. They didn't deserve to be part of this cruel plot. If he had to die trying, then he would.

The sandy-haired man glared at Wyatt, assessing his words. "Check their bags," he finally said to the scar-faced fellow. "And you," he aimed the gun at Levi's head. "Sit down. And don't say a word. Remember who's waiting for you back at the house."

Levi took the chair closest to him, easing down onto it slowly, as if waiting for it to break beneath his weight. But it held. Wyatt assumed the man must be referring to Cat. Were they holding her hostage? Some kind of sick insurance to make sure Levi didn't escape. Wyatt ground his teeth together. If he ever got out of this, he would make these men pay.

Wyatt glanced at the sandy-haired man, studying his body language, trying to decide if he had any chance at disarming the guy. He held the gun with a loose disinterest, sometimes pointing it at Levi, sometimes at Wyatt. He seemed overly blasé about the whole situation, but that was a façade. With that persuasive grin and illusion of ineptitude, he was hiding a true killer inside.

Almost imperceptibly, Levi gave a shake of his head. His message was obvious; don't try anything.

Everyone watched in silence as scar-face tipped first

Wyatt's backpack, then Stella's upside down, emptying the contents onto the dusty floor. He pawed through the mess, checking each of the small pockets, before he finally turned to the Southerner and shook his head, then went back to his position in the shadows.

"What have you done with them, you little fuck?" The Southerner asked in a low voice. "I'm not playing around anymore."

"I've done nothing, I promise. You have to believe us. All we wanted was to get the hell out of there." Wyatt crossed his fingers behind his back and prayed. If he could get these thugs to release Stella and Levi, that'd be a win. Then if he could make them follow him into the forest, maybe, just maybe, he might be able to gain the upper hand. Although, exactly how he was going to defeat two armed men, he had no idea.

Stella spoke up for the first time. "He's telling the truth… We're telling the truth." Her voice was high-pitched and wobbly as she poked her head around his bicep. She was obviously completely out of her depth, had encountered nothing like this before. And why would she have? No normal person had to deal with drug cartels and stolen diamonds. He tried to push her back behind him, but she resisted. Even while he admired her guts at speaking up, he wished she'd stayed quiet.

"We wanted nothing to do with Tony or his gems. We still don't. All we want is to be set free. We don't want any part of what you're doing here. You can have your stupid diamonds, we'll tell you where they are, just let us go."

The Southerner's eyes lit up as he studied Stella, and Wyatt pushed her more forcefully behind him, willing her to say no more, to go back to being invisible.

"What do you want me to do, Samuel? Shall I search her?" The Chechen took a few steps toward them, his lips taking on a sinister sneer. Everything inside Wyatt tensed.

"Your little woman here seems quite determined. She's kinda cute, if you like the outdoorsy type. But I think I'm inclined to believe her, more than I believe you."

Wyatt searched his memory banks for any mention of the name Samuel regarding Dmytro and his men. But nothing came up. He'd never heard of him before. Which didn't surprise him, as he'd not been a party to Dmytro's innermost sanctum. This man was clearly intelligent, a dangerous foe.

"Get them both to empty their pockets," Samuel said thoughtfully.

Wyatt had to force himself to unclench his fists. It wouldn't do for the Chechen to see he'd rattled him; that he was prepared to fight for Stella's honor. Stella was already doing as she been asked, turning her pockets inside out, tipping out balled-up tissues, a flashlight, and a couple of pieces of gum. Her hands were shaking, her lips pulled back in determined defiance.

"Search him." Samuel's command surprised Wyatt. *Damn*. It didn't take the other man long to undercover the blade hidden beneath his trouser leg. The Chechen held it up for Samuel to see.

"I thought so." The Southerner had turned the charm on again, that mischievous smile cracking open the dimples in his cheeks. "Naughty boy," he scolded.

Wyatt lifted his shoulders in a half-shrug, as if to say *you found me out*.

Levi watched everything with dark and thoughtful eyes, still not saying a word. Wyatt wondered what was going on in his brother's head. Was he being truly compliant? Or was he cooking up an escape plan behind that shuttered gaze? He speculated again what threat Samuel had used to keep Wyatt cooperating. It sounded like there was at least one more man holding Cat hostage back at the house. Perhaps all it would take was a phone call from Samuel and then Cat...

"Are you going to let us go now?" Stella's hopeful voice broke the silence.

"No, you silly girl. Did you honestly think it was that simple?" Samuel smiled at her beguilingly. "So, here's the plan. Your man here, Wyatt, will lead Fedire—Samuel nodded in the Chechen's direction—and Mike to the diamonds. And I'll stay here and keep you and the brother company until you come back." His glittering gaze turned to Wyatt. "Fair warning. Don't be too long, Mr. Wilson, I don't like to be kept waiting. I get an itchy trigger finger when I'm impatient."

Stella's frightened stare met his. This wasn't what he'd been hoping for at all.

CHAPTER SEVENTEEN

Stella sank to her knees on the dusty floor, her legs no longer able to hold her weight. She was exhausted, her bones felt like they were made of jelly. This man had no right to do this to her. To them. She couldn't stay here another minute, she couldn't. All her strength seeped out of her at that horrible man's words. She wanted to curl into a tiny ball on the dirty floorboards and pretend none of this was happening.

She'd stayed strong for so long. Stayed strong for Wyatt. But now... She had no spirit left.

Even though the freezing wind was less inside, the house was nevertheless extremely cold. This room was still mostly intact, but half the roof was missing. There wasn't even any glass in any of the windows, for God's sake, and the snow had blown straight in, forming little drifts in the corners.

"You can't..." She stopped, unable to get the words out. Licking her dry lips, she tried again. "You can't do this to us. We're innocent. You have to let us go."

"Oh, she's so precious, isn't she?" The man called Samuel smiled at her. He actually smiled. As if he hadn't a care in the world. "She's very pretty, I'll give you that. But she won't get very far if she isn't in touch with reality. I'm not sure she's right for you, Wyatt."

What was he talking about? He knew nothing about her. Knew nothing about Wyatt, either. How dare he pass judgment on her like that? She wanted to snarl at him like a feral cat. If she'd had the strength, she would've ripped at his face with her fingernails, scratched his eyeballs out. But at least the patronizing shit had achieved one thing. The anger now zinging through her veins had replaced the terror and lethargy.

"She has nothing to do with any of this. If you let her go, I promise—"

"You're not in any position to make promises," Samuel snapped.

Wyatt leaned over her protectively. She reached out and grabbed his hand, getting slowly to her feet.

"You do what you have to do," she said to Wyatt. She hoped he was going to kill the dark-haired man with the pockmarked face still pointing his gun at them, the same as he'd killed the other one up on the mountain. It was a terrible thought. A horrible idea, to take another man's life. Her compassion was at zero, however, and she no longer cared.

"I'll be okay. Levi and I will wait right here for you." She made it sound like they were going to sit around and chat with a cup of warm cocoa in their hands. As if everything was going to be fine. Wyatt needed to be on top of his game. If he thought she was accepting of all this, then who knew, he might come back to them alive. A need to touch Wyatt, to feel some of that immense strength one last time, overwhelmed her. He needed to know she trusted him. She stood on tiptoe and kissed him on the lips. Cupped his face in her palm.

She half-expected him to push her away, but his mouth softened and claimed hers.

"Oi, that's enough," Samuel shouted.

She wanted to ignore the prick, but Wyatt tensed. Letting hips lips slide away, Stella looked up into those wonderful, dark eyes. She could get lost in them. Drown in their depths for days on end. For a split second, it was as if only the two of them existed. She wasn't sure how she would cope if Wyatt didn't come back. A piece of her heart would be forever missing.

This thought had her pursing her lips. It wasn't just a piece of her heart; she wasn't surprised to discover that Wyatt owned her whole heart. She'd been slowly but inexorably captivated by him over the past few weeks. Last night in the tent had merely cemented the fact they were so right for each other. It proved their unbridled passion was a match for their soul's desire.

"I'll see you again, soon," she whispered.

"You can count on it."

Then Fedire was poking a gun in Wyatt's ribs, pushing him back to the kitchen. Wyatt eyed the man astutely, but said nothing. Even Stella could see Fedire wasn't dressed properly for a hike up the mountain. His large, black overcoat, that made him look like exactly what he was—one of those mafia-type men you read about in spy novels—might be warm because it was made of wool, but the coat draped past his knees; it'd definitely drag him down when he hit deeper snow. His shoes were shiny lace-ups. Completely wrong for the terrain he was about to encounter. But all these things gave Wyatt an advantage. And while it hardly trumped the gun the man had pointed at Wyatt's back, he needed any benefit he could get.

The second man, the one with the disfiguring scar on his neck, strolled over to join them. He was no better dressed, but he had an air of menace about him that sent Stella's blood running cold.

"It's a three-hour hike back up to the body," Wyatt said smoothly. "We won't be back before dark."

That was a lie. It'd taken them well over three hours to get down this morning. Admittedly, after killing Anton, they'd slowed their rate of descent, no longer dreading an attack from behind. It'd take them longer to climb up. Did Wyatt feel half as exhausted by their stumbling race down the mountain as she did? How was he going to cope with trekking all the way back up there again? She hoped he still had something left in his reserves, somewhere.

The diamonds were not with Tony, but Wyatt was spinning that line to make the other men believe him. She and Wyatt had buried the stones to keep them safe. It was a compromise. Stella wanted to throw them away, Wyatt wanted to keep them. Was Wyatt going to hand the diamonds over to these men? And if he did, what would happen to him?

What would happen to her and Levi?

"It's okay, I've got nowhere else to be right now. And neither do these two. Just make sure you're back before eight o'clock tonight. Otherwise... Well, you know what I mean." Samuel smirked at Wyatt.

"You think this is a good idea, boss?" Fedire glanced swiftly at Levi and then Stella. "Surely, it'll only take one of us to escort him." He jabbed his chin in Wyatt's direction. "And one of us should stay here with you."

"You keep a sharp eye on this one, you shouldn't underestimate him," Samuel told Fedire, narrowing his eyes at Wyatt. "I can handle these two, don't worry about that."

Fedire didn't seem to agree with his boss's mandate, and was perhaps going to argue again, when Samuel cut him off. "Mike, make sure you move that truck. Hide it good, now, won't you?" He threw a set of keys at the scarred man. She *had* thought it a little strange that Levi would leave his car out in the open like that. They were supposed to be meeting in secret.

The trio disappeared through the door.

It was going to be a long afternoon of waiting and wondering.

"Well, isn't this cozy, just the three of us." Samuel's breezy drawl was beginning to grate on Stella, making her dislike him intensely. "I tell you what, sugar, make yourself useful and tie up your friend here." He pointed his weapon in her direction as an extra incentive when she hesitated.

Stella threaded her way around the mess of their upturned packs scattered all over the floor and reluctantly took a roll of duct tape from Samuel's fingers.

"Sorry," she said as she approached Levi.

He lifted an eyebrow. "Not your fault."

No, it wasn't, but it didn't mean she had to like it.

"Make sure you do him up nice and tight, now," Samuel's sing-song voice came from behind. "I'll be checking your work when you've finished, and if I find he's loose, well, I'll have to find another way to keep him restrained." Stella didn't appreciate the underlying hint of menace in the blonde man's tone. He was a bastard.

"Is Cat okay?" she asked, stepping around the chair and beginning the task of taping Levi's hands together behind his back. How dare they harm her friend?

Levi's features darkened, and she felt his forearms tense beneath the tape as she wrapped it around his wrists. "I fucking hope so." He glanced up at the man with the gun. "They better not hurt her anymore. Or I'll…" Levi sputtered, lost for words.

Samuel stood over them, watching Stella to make sure she secured Levi tightly, but he didn't interrupt their conversation. It was almost as if he were listening in with voyeuristic glee.

"Where is she?" Stella asked, wondering how these thugs had managed to abduct Cat if she'd been staying at Stargazer.

"At home. We stayed in a spare guest cabin last night. But I needed to go feed Rekker. We thought we'd be safe; we were only going to be five minutes. But these bastards were lying in wait for us."

"A rather long wait it was, too," Samuel said. "Quite chilly, spending all night in that car. But our patience paid off, in the end."

Levi sneered at the Southerner and strained against his bindings.

"Make sure they're secure now, sugar," Samuel reminded her.

Wyatt continued, "I went out to the yard to feed Rekker and when I came back into the kitchen, this asshole had Cat by the neck. I refused to tell him anything, and so did Cat."

Stella could almost imagine the scene in their kitchen. Cat was a tough woman. Feisty and resolute, she wouldn't let anyone dominate her. She was probably swearing at Samuel like a hissing, spitting feral feline.

"When I wouldn't tell them where you were, this asshole got the other one, Fedire, to break Cat's little finger. I heard the snap. And she screamed..." Levi drew in a sharp breath. Stella laid a hand on his shoulder. It must've pierced him right through the heart, the sound of the woman he loved in pain. She didn't blame him for giving away their position. She would've done the same thing, if it'd been Wyatt.

She stopped what she was doing. That was the second time today she'd thought about Wyatt like that. That she would give anything to keep him safe. Was she falling for him? In love with him?

"He threatened to do it to all of her fingers, one by one, until I told him what he wanted to know," Levi continued, breaking into her wandering thoughts.

"I don't condone needless violence," Samuel said nonchalantly. "But I have a job to do. You understand how it goes."

Merde, she hated this man with a passion. Her mind was racing, and she wondered if Levi's was doing the same. Could she possibly outwit him? Could they somehow escape and help Wyatt?

"I think that's enough to hold his arms. You can start with his legs, now," Samuel directed. Stella fixed him with a stare that would melt steel, but he merely smiled back. Finally, she moved in front of the chair and knelt down beside Levi's feet.

"And that's how we found you, sugar. Simple, really. All we need is the diamonds, and everyone can go back to living their sweet little lives."

Why did Stella not believe him? Kneeling on the floor, she wrapped the tape around Levi's ankles, while surreptitiously casting her gaze around, looking for inspiration. Something, anything she could use as a tool or a weapon. The discarded items from their backpacks were scattered everywhere, pushed aside as Mike sorted through them. Nothing. There was nothing she could use. It was useless. They were going to die at the hand of this man and his thugs. Her normally nimble fingers struggled to continue wrapping the tape as her hands shook.

That's when she spotted it. A lighter. The red plastic winking at her through the gloom. Lying on the floor a few feet away. It must've been in Wyatt's pack; she remembered him using it to start their campfires.

"You're not really going to let us go, are you?" she asked, tipping her head up to look Samuel in the eyes. "As soon as Wyatt gets back, you're going to kill us all." It wasn't hard to add a hint of hysteria to her voice. "I don't want to die. You can't kill us," she wailed, flopping backward onto her butt on the floor and then toppling over.

Levi shot her a look that was half confused, half anguished. Good, if he believed her, then so would Samuel. She lay on the floor and rolled onto her side, one hand covering her face as she moaned louder and louder. Her other hand snaked out, feeling around blindly. Then she had it. The lighter was secreted in her palm as she drew her arm back.

"Calm down, sugar," Samuel crooned, taking a step toward her.

"Don't come near me," she yelled. "Don't you touch me."

"All right," he said, raising his hands above his head. "But you need to settle down."

"Stella, it's okay. We'll be fine." Levi's concerned look was exactly right; it played perfectly into her little game. "Come over here," he entreated.

Stella got up from the floor, pretending to wipe away tears, taking a wide berth around Samuel. She reached Levi and flung her arms around his shoulders, sobbing into his neck. "They are, Levi. They're going to kill us, I know it."

Levi made soothing noises. Dipping one hand lower behind his back, she slipped the lighter into Levi's bound hands, and prayed he'd know what to do with it. The small flame would hopefully burn through the plastic duct tape. If he could get it lit, with his wrists tied together as they were. He stiffened ever so slightly, but immediately went back to making his mollifying sounds of comfort.

"All right, you're fine now. Get away from him. Fucking hysterical women." Samuel snorted. "Always have to make a scene." Samuel was pointing the gun at her again, and she knew she was walking a fine line. She didn't want to get him too riled up.

Making sniffling sounds, she finally stepped away from Levi, hiding her face from Samuel, as if trying to get herself together. If it took a scene to get them out of here, then she was prepared to degrade herself and do just about anything.

She glanced sideways at Levi, and he gave an imperceptible nod. He was in on her plan. Now all she had to do was distract Samuel long enough that he wouldn't notice what Levi was up to.

"I'm cold," she complained, still swiping at her face.

"So am I. Can't believe Dmytro sent us to this freezing hellhole. But there ain't much I can do about that, sugar." Samuel grinned.

Stella took a few steps away from Levi. "Isn't that a fireplace over there?" She pointed toward the far wall. Samuel came closer, looking in the direction she was pointing. His back was now to Levi.

"What are you, stupid? We can't light a fire, someone would see the smoke," he growled.

"But I'm cold," she whined again. "What if we stuff something up the chimney, to stop the smoke going up it?" She walked toward the fireplace, praying he'd follow. He did. "We could set some of these clothes alight." She gathered up handfuls of apparel from the floor.

Samuel gazed at the fireplace for a few seconds, considering. He must be cold, to actually be evaluating her foolish idea. She'd plucked it out of the recesses of her brain. If she were Samuel, there was no way she'd light a fire. Of course, it'd attract attention; smoke coming from an abandoned farmhouse.

Levi made no sound behind them, but suddenly she got the faint whiff of burning plastic. Quick, she needed another distraction. She rushed forward, shoving her armful into the old fireplace, which was full of cobwebs and snow drifts.

"Stop that, right now," Samuel demanded. The gun was back up and pointing directly at her.

Unexpectedly, there was a loud thump from behind them. Both she and Samuel turned their heads in surprise, and saw Levi lying sideways on the floor. His hands were free, and he was curled over his knees, doing something to his ankles. Stella knew he was probably burning through his bindings. But the thug still had no idea what was going on.

Samuel swung around to face Levi, his gun hand coming up.

Stella did the only thing she could think of; she kicked at Samuel's hand that held the gun. Wonder of wonders, the weapon went flying, Samuel was taken completely by surprise, not expecting her to attack.

He recovered in an instant, and with a bellow of rage, he grabbed her by the throat and sent her crashing to the floor.

CHAPTER EIGHTEEN

Wyatt ran as fast and as hard as he could, heart hammering loudly in his ears. He had to get back to Stella. Fedire was dead, that much he knew for sure. But Mike? He wasn't so convinced about him. Wyatt had definitely shot him. Heard the thud of the bullet imbedding in his skin, and the oof sound as the air left his lungs when he was driven backward, over the edge of the steep ravine. But that didn't mean he was dead. Or even out of action.

As Wyatt had led the two thugs away from the ruined house, he'd bided his time, studied his two foes with covert, sideways glances to try to decide which one was more dangerous. Fedire seemed to be Samuel's favorite. But to Wyatt's highly attuned instincts, it was Mike who struck him as the more treacherous of the two.

In the first few minutes after they left the house, Wyatt had racked his brain, trying to remember as much of the terrain as he could. He'd only walked this trail once since he'd been living at Levi's and then he and Stella had come down the hard way this morning, straight through the untamed forest.

There was a rocky plateau about a mile up into the foothills, Wyatt saw it clearly in his mind's eye. It'd be far enough distant from the house so that hopefully they wouldn't hear a gunshot, if it came to that. But not so far that it'd take too long for him to run back. On one side, there was a sharp drop-off, and the plateau itself contained piles of boulders, left over from millions of years ago, perhaps when a river had run through the area. The rocks would give him cover, help to confuse his foes if he needed to run for it. The snow would still be in deep drifts after the blizzard, as there was little tree cover. An idea was forming, even as they walked.

Wyatt would not lead them to the diamonds. He wasn't climbing back up this mountain today; not if he could help it. He had to return to Stella; make sure she was safe.

They walked in silence—Wyatt had no desire to converse with these men—him in the lead, Fedire behind him and Mike bringing up the rear.

Wyatt doubted Samuel was a man of his word, but he hoped against hope that he'd keep Stella and Levi alive, at least until the diamonds were returned. But many unanswered questions bounced around in his head. Would he be too late? Had Samuel killed Levi and Stella already? It did no good to keep thinking these things, it only distracted him from the task in front of him. But he was so terrified. What if he was doing this all for nothing?

He was already bone-weary from the middle-of-the-night fight to the death and then their morning march down the mountain. But he forced himself to go faster.

It took them a little over twenty minutes to reach the plateau. All the while, Wyatt watched the two men behind him and planned. The first thing he needed was to separate them. His odds were improved one-on-one. Extending his stride, he put distance between him and Fedire. The swarthy man was trying to hide how out of breath he was; his big woolen coat weighing him down and those stupid shoes slipping in the snow. It wasn't hard for Wyatt to put ten, and then twenty yards between them as Fedire concentrated on the rough terrain. By the time the other man looked up and gave a shout, it was too late. Wyatt had reached the first pile of boulders.

He launched himself forward, sprinting behind the cover of the rocks. There was a loud crack as Mike fired a shot, but it pinged harmlessly off the stones. Wyatt twisted and turned, racing through the maze of craggy clefts and broken boulders. The two men shouted at him to stop, but their voices were muffled, and they soon faded as he clambered up the ever-increasing slope. At last, Wyatt scooted behind the cover of an outcrop, bending over to regain his breath.

He'd wait here.

He was sweating from exertion, and removed his knit cap and gloves, but knew it would be suicide to take off his coat. As quietly as he could, he climbed the rocky formation. He needed to see the lay of the land. If he was lucky, he might even spot one of the thugs.

Lying flat on his stomach, he peered over the edge. He was around twenty feet off the ground. It was now early afternoon but dark clouds had scudded in to cover the sun and the day was gray and cheerless, adding to the eerie feeling in beneath the gloom of the fir trees. Wyatt's stomach growled; he hadn't had time to eat anything all day. He ignored the complaint from his belly.

A noise below alerted him, and he held his breath.

Fedire crept stealthily into view, gun pointed and at the ready as he hunted Wyatt. Mike was nowhere to be seen. Hopefully, they'd split up to search for him, exactly as he'd envisaged. Soon, Fedire was directly below him.

Wyatt had no way of knowing where Mike was. He listened intently, but could hear nothing to indicate the other man was nearby. It was now or never; if he didn't take this chance, he might not get another one. Bracing himself, he took a deep breath, pushed up to a crouch and then launched himself, hitting his target head-on.

Landing on Fedire broke his fall. He and Fedire tumbled together over the snowy ground. Wyatt had been aiming to knock the gun out of the other man's hand. Unfortunately, he'd missed his mark, and now it was a wrestle for domination of the weapon.

It was a strange fight, with lots of grunting and straining, both men intently fixed on gaining control of the gun. Wyatt had one knee hooked around Fedire's waist, one hand pinning his free arm behind him, and the other locked on the wrist holding the gun. They were in a checkmate.

Wyatt gathered all his remaining strength, raised himself up slightly, and head-butted Fedire in the nose. At the same time, he smashed the man's arm repeatedly on the ground. Suddenly, the weapon skidded across the muddy ground, away from both of them.

Wyatt was momentarily distracted, and Fedire pushed him off, sending him tumbling. Fedire began to crawl toward the weapon.

There was a large rock on the ground nearby. Wyatt picked it up and hurled himself toward Fedire. Raising the rock, he brought it down on Fedire's hand, just as his fingers grazed the handle of the pistol. The other man howled in pain and rolled away. Wyatt raised the rock again. This time bringing it down on Fedire's unprotected head.

It made a horrible, wet, cracking sound and Wyatt looked away. When he found the courage to look back, Fedire's eyes were open, staring up at the sky as he lay completely still.

Wyatt shuffled backwards across the dirt until his spine came to rest against the rock face.

This was the second man he'd killed today.

He tried to regulate his breathing, glanced away from the dead man lying in the forest.

His job wasn't finished, however. Had the sound of fighting alerted Mike to their position?

With a great effort of will, Wyatt got to his feet. He picked up the gun and stumbled away from the small clearing.

Which direction had Mike gone? He began a sneaking, methodical search back the way they'd come, gun at the ready. Should he perhaps return to the house? Run back and hope he got there before Mike tracked him down?

He was adjacent to where the ravine dropped away from the brink of the plateau; close to rejoining the trail. The tree cover thinned out, and he was about to turn and make a dash down the trail, when the snap of a twig alerted him.

Mike appeared from behind a large trunk. He looked nearly as surprised as Wyatt, clearly not having heard him coming. They both raised their guns, but Wyatt got his round off a millisecond before Mike. He ducked and felt the whiz of a bullet pass close by. He saw Mike spin away and then he was gone, tumbling down the steep slope into the ravine.

Now Wyatt was running as fast as his battered body would allow. To get back to Stella.

The gray clouds had gotten darker, holding the promise of snow. But he was nearly there, his feet pounding along the trail of snowy footprints they'd left only half an hour ago. He should stop on the outskirts, hunker down behind the same bush to scout out the place. Make sure he wasn't about to be gunned down as he ran up the pathway. But he kept going, he had to see for himself. Desperation drove him on.

Common sense finally prevailed, and when he reached the back door, he slowed down enough to take a few deep breaths. Slipping through the doorway, gun held at the ready, he steeled himself for what he might find.

The scene before him was so incomprehensible it took his mind a few seconds to adjust.

Stella was standing in the middle of the living room, using

her hands to accentuate her words as she talked. Levi was also in the room, stuffing things back into Wyatt's backpack. It took a second for Wyatt to locate Samuel. He was strapped to a chair in the corner, wrapped up like a Christmas present, with duct tape over his mouth.

He didn't know how they'd done it, but they'd managed to overpower Dmytro's right-hand man. Stella was very much alive. And very much as gorgeous as ever.

"Stella," he said softly. She didn't hear him, she was too busy talking.

"But we have to go after him," she declared, her voice full of anguish. "Those men will kill him as soon as he hands over the diamonds."

"I agree with you, Stella, and that's why I'm going. But you need to stay here and wait for the police. You need to—" Levi swung around to face Stella and caught sight of Wyatt standing in the doorway. His face split into a huge grin.

Stella whirled around. "Wyatt? You're here. You're safe." She ran to him and threw herself against his chest. "Are you okay? Are you hurt?"

"I'm fine," he murmured, resting his nose in her neck, inhaling her scent. "I'm fine." They held each other for uncounted seconds as he let the desperate fear ebb out of him.

Levi came up and patted him on the back. "Good to see you in one piece. We were worried about you."

"And I was worried about you. I came back to rescue you, but it looks like you had it all sorted." Wyatt didn't release Stella from his arms, but he dragged his bother to join in their embrace for a few seconds before releasing him.

"Yes, thanks to Stella, here. She's wasted as a pastry chef, I'm telling you. She needs to join the secret service, or the FBI, something like that," Levi joked.

"How did you…?" Wyatt waved a hand, encompassing the

whole room. Samuel glared daggers at him from his chair.

Stella and Levi began talking at once, and Wyatt had to smile over their garbled conversation. They stopped talking, and all laughed. It was an odd sound, echoing around the ruined house. But it felt good, a release of tension and stress.

"How about we tell you later," Levi said. "Sheriff Buchanan is on his way to my house. I need to know Cat is safe and Jude is keeping me posted. Once he's rescued her, he's promised to come and pick up the trash over here." Levi held up a cell phone. "I've borrowed Samuel's, seeing as how he confiscated mine." He patted his coat pocket. "I've also *borrowed* his gun, just in case you're wondering where it got to. I'll go and give the sheriff an update, tell him you're safe."

"Good idea." Wyatt murmured, lowering his chin back onto the top of Stella's head. Once Levi disappeared through the front door to make his call, he dipped his head to kiss Stella, not caring that Samuel was glaring at them from his chair.

Her lips were soft and glorious. A balm to his wounded soul. He'd been so sure he was going to come into this room to find her dead. It was hard to believe she was here, in his arms. But she was real, the way her fingernails dug into the back of his neck, pulling him down so her lips could reach his, proved that. The little satisfied noise she made deep in her throat as he delved into her mouth with his tongue was also real. That small sound had him going all mushy inside, as if something was melting in his chest.

He could hardly believe all they'd been through. And he could hardly believe the emotions ripping through his chest. Powerful emotions that threatened to swamp him. Were they borne from the hardship they'd endured? Their forced intimacy on the hike over the hills? He didn't think so. Wyatt had recognized there was something special about Stella from the very first time he'd laid eyes on her. His attraction had intensified when they were caught together in that blizzard and spent the night in his truck. She was so different to anyone else he'd ever known. The chunk of his heart that'd been wounded by Zoe's death and then his false incarceration became whole again when she was around. He no longer felt as if he was an outsider, doomed to live a lonely, tormented life.

The word *love* hovered in his mind. Was this what it was like to be in love with a woman? He'd been expecting fireworks and shooting stars, but this was something much more tender, but also painfully exquisite. It'd crept up on him. She made him feel unbroken again.

Her lips were melded to his, and he funneled all his yearning into her. It was enough right now to kiss her. Although his body wanted more, his erection throbbing against the zipper of his pants, his mind soaked up this familiarity of her kiss, taking it to his heart and locking it inside. He decided he was never letting her go. They could stay like this forever.

It was an impossible task, however. There were so many things that needed to be done, so many things that needed to be said. The moment would have to be broken. Cat was still in danger. He needed to know she was safe before he fully relaxed. There was also Mike. He might yet be a threat to them all; they needed to be on the lookout. Most likely he was dead at the bottom of the ravine, or if he was still alive, he'd hightailed it out of there. Although, where he'd go in that wilderness was anyone's guess.

As if Stella could sense the change in him, she withdrew her lips and stepped out of his arms.

"I'm glad you're safe," she said with a beatific smile. "We can talk about the rest later."

He nodded in agreement, relieved she understood him so completely.

"I'll see if I can get all our stuff in our backpacks," she suggested, and knelt down to retrieve the one Levi had been stuffing things into earlier.

"Hey, Levi." He started after his brother, wanting to ask about Cat, as well as warn him about Mike, make sure he reported him to the sheriff.

A movement to his left caught his eye.

He spun around, reaching for the gun nestled in his coat pocket, while stepping back toward Stella.

Mike was there.

He raised his weapon.

And aimed.

Not at him, but at Stella.

"Stella," he shouted. She looked up from where she knelt on the floor and smiled, not realizing the danger. He couldn't let her die. He hadn't been able to save Zoe, but he could save her.

He got off a single shot as he dived in front of Stella. It all happened in the blink of an eye.

Pain ripped through his chest as he crashed onto the wooden floorboards.

CHAPTER NINETEEN

Stella sat by Wyatt's bedside, one hand entwined with his on top of the covers. Her eyes were scratchy and raw from lack of sleep—it was nearly midnight—but she couldn't close them. Wyatt was going to be okay; all the doctors had promised her that. So why wouldn't he wake up? She needed him to wake up, hold her tight, and tell her he was fine.

Cat and Levi had been there until recently. Stella couldn't put into words how joyful she'd been when she saw Cat walk, unaided, into the hospital. She had yet to hear the story of her friend's full encounter with Dmytro's thugs, but that could wait until tomorrow. All that mattered was she was safe, and she had Levi by her side. Cat's broken finger had been splinted to the one next to it, and she was acting as if nothing had happened. They'd gone home to get some rest, after the doctors assured them many, many times that Wyatt would be fine. It'd do them both the world of good to cocoon themselves in bed, perhaps make love and reconnect after their terrifying ordeal. Let all the poison of the recent few days drain away. If only she and Wyatt could do the same.

Stella stared out the window, the lights of Missoula twinkling back at her. Her mind drifted back to this afternoon. But it shied away from all the violence and death.

She knew she'd have to deal with it eventually, but not tonight, not while she was waiting for Wyatt to come back to her.

He'd saved her life. Had dived in front of the bullet without a moment's thought. She hadn't known what was happening until it was too late. Until the sound of gunfire echoed in her ears and Wyatt lay on the floor bleeding.

The man called Mike also lay on the floor. Wyatt had shot him, even as he was racing to save her. Then Levi appeared in the doorway, a gun in his hand. When Mike tried to get up, Levi had shouted at him, told him to stay where he was and then stood over him with the gun pointed in his face.

Stella had crawled across the floor to Wyatt, and he'd actually smiled up at her. As if he'd done a great thing. She wanted to yell at him, tell him he was a fool. Instead, it was as if she been taken over by some survivalist instinct. Pulling his coat open, she'd rolled him over, ignoring his cries of pain, and surveyed the wound. It was high on the right-hand side of his back, beneath his armpit. There was a lot of blood. She grabbed one of the bits of clothing scattered on the floor, and used it to staunch the injury, pressing down hard.

"*Idiot*," she mumbled to herself. "*Imbécile*." She kept repeating the phrase over and over. How could he have done something so stupid?

"I love it when you speak French," Wyatt had murmured, gaze fixed on her.

She ignored him. Her only aim was to keep him alive. If he was fool enough to try to throw away his own life, then she would have to be the one to save it for him. Because she wanted him to live.

She wanted to be part of his life, if he would have her. If these three days together had taught her one thing, it was that Wyatt Wilson was a worthy man. He'd stolen her heart.

Later on, the doctors told her the bullet had ricocheted off a rib. He was lucky on two counts. The rib had deflected the slug, leaving a shallow wound beneath the fleshy part of his arm. And he was also lucky that when the rib cracked, none of the broken pieces had pierced his lung. They'd taken him into surgery to remove the bits of shattered bone, and stitch up the wound, but said he would be up and about in a few days' time.

She had known none of that at the time, however, all she'd seen was blood seeping everywhere, and when the ambulance had finally arrived, she begged to be allowed to ride with him, terrified he was going to die on the way to the hospital.

A groan from the bed beside her brought her back to the room.

"Wyatt? I'm here."

He groaned again, his eyelids fluttering. She squeezed his hand, and he squeezed back.

"You're in the hospital. But you're going to be okay."

Wyatt struggled to open his eyes. He rolled his head on the pillow and licked his lips. Water, he must need some water. She turned to snag the plastic cup on the bedside table.

When she turned back, his dark eyes were open and fixed on her. She never thought she would be so happy to stare into someone else's eyes. So inky they were like an obsidian lake. Definitely the windows to his soul. Because she could see his whole essence bared before her, now. She wanted to dive into the mysterious lake that was Wyatt.

"I don't care about me. What about you?" he croaked.

She gave an exasperated sigh. "*Zut*. Why are you so worried about me, when you're the one lying in the hospital bed? I'm great, can't you see?" She let go of his hand and did a little twirl.

"That's good. Very good," he mumbled. But he looked sad. What was going on in his head?

Pushing the covers aside, she climbed carefully onto the bed, lying on the opposite side of his injured chest. Snuggling down into the cook of his arm, she reveled in the feel of his firm body against hers. At first, he tensed, then he gave a deep sigh—she hoped that was of contentment—and shifted his arm so it draped around her neck, tucking her in closer.

"You feel nice. This feels good. But you shouldn't be here. You need to go home."

"I'm not going anywhere." Stella curled her leg over the top of his, snuggling even deeper, resting her hand lightly on his abdomen. She could feel his wonderfully chiseled abs beneath the thin, cotton blanket. She was happy he was awake, happy to lie next to him.

"Well, you should. You should want to get as far away from me as possible."

What was he saying? She brought her head up so she could stare at his profile. But he wouldn't meet her gaze. "Why would you think that?" She pursed her lips and narrowed her eyes at him.

"Because I'm not good for you. I'm a dangerous influence. Bad things happen when I'm around."

"*Merde.* Don't be *le idiot*," she said, slipping into French once more. "You are a good man. Full of spirit and life. You're passionate about your land. I can see what you are, beneath that big, gruff exterior you put on. You are as soft as a teddy bear inside. Like one of my profiteroles. Hard and crusty on the outside, but creamy and sweet on the inside. Bad things have happened to you, but *you* are not a bad man. You don't frighten me, Wyatt." She could feel him considering her words, but he wouldn't look at her.

"You should be afraid," he said so gently, she almost didn't hear him. "I'm afraid."

"Afraid of what?"

He hesitated, staring out the window. She gave him the

time he needed to form his answer, because this was the crux of his problem.

"Myself," he finally answered.

"What do you mean?"

"I'm afraid I might hurt you inadvertently. I wouldn't intend to do it, but I would anyway."

"You did the exact opposite this afternoon," she said, half rising on her elbow, so she could make her point. "You saved me. You put yourself in danger so I wouldn't get hurt. That's how I know you'd never harm me. I trust you, Wyatt, even when you don't trust yourself."

"That was... Well, it was different. I did that because..."

She knew why he'd done it, but would he ever admit it to himself?

"It was my fault you were in that situation in the first place. If it hadn't been for me, you'd be safely tucked up in the Stargazer kitchen, cooking up one of your amazing dishes."

He was still harping on about this whole diamond thing. How could she make him see she didn't blame him for any of this? He'd only ever been trying to protect her.

"Would it make any difference if I said I'm falling in love with you?"

This got his attention. His head snapped around and his dark eyes flashed.

"Don't say that."

"Why not? It's true." She took a perverse delight in watching him squirm. It was going to be hard for him to hear the truth. Hard for him to accept it. She might have to treat him like a skittish horse for a while, with care and patience. But she knew Wyatt would come around, eventually. Because he was in love with her, too, he just had to admit it.

He stuttered, unable to form a coherent sentence as he stared at her.

"Don't worry," she crooned. "Lay your head down here." She patted the pillow, and he lay back against it, never taking his eyes from her face. "Let's sleep now. I need to sleep. With you. Here." She smothered a yawn.

His black eyes were deep as night. He opened his mouth to say something more, and she put a finger against his lips.

"Hush, Wyatt. It will all be okay, I promise."

His hand came up to cover hers as it lay on his chest, pressed it hard against his rib cage, right above his heart.

"Maybe it will," he agreed. "Maybe it will."

CHAPTER TWENTY

"Stella, hurry up, or we're going to start without you," Emily called. Wyatt glanced over his shoulder to where Stella was still fussing around in the small kitchen, cleaning up, and then winced as the movement caused pain to shoot up his side.

Tom and Emily had invited them all for a meal in their small cabin at Stargazer, to celebrate Wyatt getting out of the hospital, and the fact their ordeal had come to a—sort of— happy ending. But of course, Stella couldn't help herself and had offered to cook. Cat and Levi, Penny and Dale were also there. They were all seated on the couch or perched on dining chairs, drawn up to form a circle, with plates of food balanced on their knees. Wyatt had been given the luxury of a spot on the couch, thanks to his injuries, his left arm in a sling for at least the next few weeks.

"I'm coming," Stella sang, and then she was there, settled next to him on the couch, her leg resting against his. He drew in her scent, and his heart lifted at her presence. "You can all eat now," she said, using her fork to dig into the delicious-looking chicken dish. Before she put the food in her mouth, however, she cast him a concerned look. "Are you okay?" she whispered. She must've noticed him wince earlier.

"Yes." He nodded and then gave her a lopsided smile. Of course, he was okay, she was sitting beside him, he couldn't be better.

There were sounds of appreciation and murmurs of *this is yummy*, as people began to eat.

"There are pignoli cookies for after," Stella said.

Wyatt chucked quietly to himself. She'd made his favorites. The cookies she knew his mother used to make him. A slight flash of sorrow flickered through him, as he wondered what his mother was up to, back in Italy. He wondered if she even knew he'd spent two years in jail. Or that he'd nearly died at the hands of a drug-smuggling group of thugs? He shrugged. Perhaps she didn't care. Or perhaps she was dead, who knew.

Wyatt took a mouthful, but he couldn't keep quiet any longer. "So, did you find them?" he blurted out, staring at Levi, who sat across from him in a single recliner. He hadn't seen his brother all day, and the question had been burning a brand in his mind the whole time.

"Of course, I did," Levi snorted. Wyatt smiled. His brother was picking up Cat's habit of snorting every time someone said something he didn't like. "They were right were you said they were."

"What are they going to do with them?" Wyatt prompted.

Levi took another bite before he answered. "They'll go into evidence. Sheriff Buchanan is hoping it might be enough to set up a case against Dmytro."

Wyatt's heart lurched against the inside of his rib cage. "Even though he's in prison?" It was an outcome he'd been silently hoping for. But he knew better than most how slippery Dmytro could be.

"Yep," Levi said smugly. "This time they're going to try to get him for Bryce's murder, as well as Tony's. If they can prove he ordered his men to kill them, then he'll spend the rest of his life in jail."

Wyatt shrugged. It was a long shot. Samuel was in police custody, but he was refusing to talk, even after he was charged with aggravated kidnapping and torture. Mike was recovering in the hospital, under police guard. Wyatt doubted he'd be of much use to the police in building a case against Dmytro, either.

Wyatt really hoped it'd be enough to keep Dmytro so busy that he didn't have time to think about anything else; like retribution. Sheriff Buchanan had told him he had nothing to worry about, that he'd make sure Dmytro wouldn't cause him any problems. Bryce's murder was still under investigation. Tony never did give Wyatt a good explanation for why Bryce had been murdered. The thugs had most likely shown up at CJ's, hoping to find Wyatt. But it wasn't likely to be a case of mistaken identity. With his long beard and many tattoos, Bryce could hardly have been confused for Wyatt. Deputy Jude Wilder thought it might've been as simple as Bryce standing up to the thugs. Perhaps he'd tried to drive the two men out of his café and things had gotten heated. Poor Bryce. Wyatt could hardly believe he was dead, even now. He hadn't had time to grieve properly for his boss and mentor yet.

"And Tony? Did you find his body?"

"Yeah." A look of distaste crossed Levi's face. "Thankfully, that forecast snow held off. Another snowfall might've covered his body and we would've had to wait 'til spring to recover him."

Police had confirmed the photo being shown around by the two mysterious strangers—who'd later been identified as Fedire and Mike—was indeed of Tony. Which had obviously spooked Tony and was the reason for him being a no-show on the day he was supposed to collect his diamonds from Wyatt.

"We found the other guy, Anton, as well," Levi said.

"Which is a good thing, as it corroborates your story. Not that I ever doubted you," he added quickly. "But you know, the cops, always want to get their facts straight."

The police had taken his statement at a bedside interview, but they needed more information before they believed his sordid tale. So, Wyatt had spent most of yesterday, after they discharged him from the hospital, talking to the police and then two FBI agents. Because Dmytro was involved in all kinds of things, including drugs as well as diamond smuggling, the FBI had been called in, much to the sheriff's displeasure. They'd grilled him all day, until Wyatt was left feeling drained and it'd sparked that old resentment about his lack of fair treatment at the hand of the authorities, as he was made to feel small and somehow at fault. But Wyatt had managed to hold his tongue. Just. They'd also grilled Stella for most of the day, in a separate room, which rankled Wyatt no end. She had nothing to do with any of it. But as Levi said, they needed her story to verify his. Along with Levi and Cat's testimony, the sheriff was satisfied with Wyatt's report, and no charges were to be laid against him.

While he and Stella were being interviewed yesterday, Levi had led Deputy Wilder to where Wyatt had buried the diamonds. The sheriff was most keen to recover them. Wyatt had given Levi a detailed description of where to find them, as well as the rough coordinates he'd worked out after studying some digital maps. They were nestled in the roots of a large pine tree, covered with leaves and other forest detritus, not on Tony's body, as he'd told Samuel and his men. He and Stella had buried them to keep them safe. As their insurance, if they needed it, against Dmytro and his thugs. But he'd never, ever considered keeping them, not even for a split second. He didn't need that kind of grief. And even though the money would've been nice, he and Stella would be fine without it. More than fine.

Stella and him. The idea was still sinking in. She'd hardly left his side for the past three days. And he liked it. He glanced over and watched her face in profile as she chatted to Penny, who was sitting next to her. She was so gorgeous; it made his chest hurt whenever he looked at her.

"So, is it true? Have you guys actually set a date?" Stella called to Cat, putting Wyatt's thoughts on hold. There was a hush, as everyone waited for Cat to reply.

"Yes, we have." Cat glanced sideways at Levi, and her ears turned pink. It was unlike Cat to be unsettled by everyone's attention. "We booked in a celebrant the other day, so it's official. It's going to be the twentieth of June."

"The first day of summer," Stella sang out. Wyatt remembered telling her at the New Year's Eve party—which seemed like a million years ago—he thought it would be that day.

There was much laughter and ribbing around the room as Stella, Emily, and Penny all demanded they help Cat find a dress. They talked, and they ate chicken and pignoli cookies until no one could fit another thing in. Wyatt drew in the happiness and camaraderie. He was always going to be the introspective one who liked to listen and watch, taking in everything going on around him. That would never change. What had changed, however, was how he felt about his place in the world. He no longer felt disenfranchised. He now knew there was a place where he belonged. It was partly due to Levi and Cat's love and acceptance of him into their home and their lives. But most of this new feeling was because of Stella, and the way she made him want things again.

"Hey, bro." Levi broke into his reverie. His brother stroked his beard and looked at Wyatt askew. "I've got another interesting tidbit of news," he said quietly.

Wyatt's stomach tightened. What was his brother going to tell him now?

"Jude mentioned that Clayton had been in to see them in the sheriff's office, after he heard what'd happened."

Wyatt sat up a little straighter. He'd heard a lot about Clayton and his antics as the suspected arsonist. But their paths had crossed for a short time when he'd served with Clayton in Missoula prison while the other man had been waiting to be sentenced for his attempted abduction charges. While they'd never become friends, he'd heard the rumors shooting through the prison grapevine about what Clayton may or may not have been into. But then Wyatt was released, and he'd lost touch with Clayton. He knew he'd been let out recently. Wyatt knew a twinge of guilt. He understood what the man must be going through, fresh out of prison wasn't a great place to be in. Perhaps he should visit the guy, offer advice and a friendly smile.

"What did he want with the sheriff's office?"

"This is strictly confidential," Levi lowered his voice and leaned in closer. "It seems he might have some dirt on Dmytro. Something he found out while he was in jail and he's willing to give it to the cops, if it'll help build the case against Dmytro."

"Wow." Wyatt was momentarily lost for words. Could it be true? Dmytro had dealings with lots of people, had his finger in many pies. But why would Clayton want to help? Most of the town still hadn't forgiven him, even though he'd been acquitted of all charges on the arson attacks against the ranch. And Cat definitely hadn't forgiven him after he tried to abduct her. In some ways, Wyatt could sympathize with Clayton. He'd been accused of a crime he didn't commit. Why would he want to help, when everyone seemed to have turned against him?

"I wonder what he has on Dmytro?"

Levi lifted his shoulder in a shrug. "Jude wouldn't tell me, but he said Clayton—"

Levi stopped mid-sentence as he noticed Penny staring at them. She'd ceased listening to the other conversation about the wedding and was now concentrating on Levi and Wyatt.

Levi glared at her and she sat back in her chair, a slight frown lining her brow.

"Sorry, I shouldn't have been eavesdropping. But I always thought Clayton was a little misunderstood." The last part was said a tad defensively, and with a quick glance in Cat's direction, to make sure she wasn't listening.

Wyatt didn't know Penny well, his only interaction with her had been if he needed something at the front reception, or through Stella, as they were best friends and shared a room on the ranch. Penny was pretty. She had a pouty look to her mouth that some men might find attractive, with full, pink lips. Long, blonde hair and a killer body she liked to show off in skin-tight jeans, made her even more attractive. Tonight, she was wearing her glasses, as usual, and her hair was tied up in a long braid, giving her an almost teacher-like quality. Wyatt racked his brain to remember if she was going out with anyone. He didn't think so. Although, why a beautiful woman like her wasn't seeing anyone, was beyond him.

"Sorry," she apologized again, looking contrite. "I didn't mean to interrupt your conversation."

"Not a problem," Levi said breezily. A look passed between the two brothers, Levi letting him know they'd continue the conversation later. Then, as if something Cat had said suddenly registered, Levi asked loudly, "What did you say?"

"I'm going to ride right up to the celebrant on my motorcycle."

Levi put his head in his hands in mock dismay, and everyone laughed. Wyatt wouldn't put it past Cat to do exactly as she threatened.

Everyone had a comment about Cat rocking up on her motorcycle. Wyatt sat back and watched Stella, her hands waving excitedly in the air as she made a point. Looking at Stella, he couldn't hold back the surge of love that washed through him. Nor the surge of desire. He wanted to take her home; tell her all the things she needed to hear.

Wyatt got carefully off the couch and stood. "We're off. Stella is going to drive me home," he announced, handing his plate to a surprised Levi. He offered Stella a hand, and she stood with a giggle, handing her plate to an equally surprised Penny.

He didn't care that everyone smiled smugly at him, as if they knew exactly what he and Stella were up to. Because they'd be correct. He was going to take Stella to his bed and make love to her. It might not be the most fantastic lovemaking because of his injury, but he'd make up for that. As soon as the stitches were out and his cracked ribs healed, boy he was going to make up for it.

As they stood in the doorway, Stella ready to help him on with his coat, he stopped to stare at her. A few strands of hair had fallen out of her messy bun and he gently tucked them behind her ear. He could hardly believe this woman wanted to be with him. Since the very first moment he'd set eyes on her, he'd wanted her. But it'd been a dream, a fantasy. He'd never thought he'd ever be good enough for someone like her. But he was living proof that dreams sometimes did come true.

"See you tomorrow." Stella waved at everyone still seated in the small living room.

"Don't do anything I wouldn't do," Cat replied with a sassy grin. Stella's ears turned pink, but she returned Cat's grin with a cheeky grin of her own.

She helped him on with his coat, then they were out the door, the sound of everyone wishing them a good night ringing in their ears. Stella snuggled under his arm and they walked in silence down the gravel roadway to his truck in the parking lot.

The night was still, with not a breath of wind and not a cloud in the sky. The cold air nipped at his nose and his cheeks. More snow was forecast for later in the week, but it was as if the heavens had cleared just for them tonight. A carpet of stars hovered overhead.

Stella stopped and tipped her head back to stare at the night sky, a wisp of steam escaping her mouth as she sighed.

"It's so beautiful, Wyatt. I'm so glad I came to Montana, so I could see this." She released him and twirled around. "And I'm so glad I met you. You opened my eyes to how wondrous this all is. Before we ran away into the hills, I never truly understood. Thank you."

Was she really thanking him for dragging her into the mountains and making her pitch a camp in the snow and ice?

"I want to go back out there again, soon," she said.

He laughed loud and long. "If that's what you want, darlin', then that's what we'll do."

Three nights ago, lying next to him in his hospital bed, she'd declared she was in love with him. At the time, he'd tried to deny it; to deny her, even though he felt the veracity of her words. But she was a force of nature, and he'd finally decided that if she wouldn't leave him, then he was going to have to embrace her, wholeheartedly, welcome her into his life and into his heart.

It was his turn, now.

"Stella."

"Hmm," she murmured, head back, still watching the stars.

He touched her chin with his thumb and stepped in close, pulling her into his embrace with his good arm. Sensing he had something important to say, she withdrew her gaze from the stars, locking it on him, instead.

"I spent my whole life never really feeling like I fitted in. I agree, I probably had a chip on my shoulder, thought I had something to prove. And when I ended up in jail, it merely demonstrated to me what I already knew; that I'd never amount to anything. I was so hurt and resented everyone and everything. Then you came along." He paused, breathing in deeply, feeling his chest expand as the weight of the words lifted away from him. "I wasn't sure I would ever say this again. I'm in love with you, Stella."

"I know," she said with a grin. "Isn't it fantastic?" She stood on tiptoe and kissed him, long and deep. "Come on," she said, tugging him by the hand. "I need to get you naked."

His future now looked bright. Much brighter than it had even a week ago. He couldn't wait to start making memories with her.

EPILOGUE

Even wearing black, Stella looked stunning. Wyatt admired the way she sat, straight-backed and decorous in one of Levi's armchairs. She was wearing a simple black, knit dress in honor of the day, but it clung to her curves in all the right places, revealing her sinuous hips and highlighting her pert, but magnificent breasts. And hadn't he had enormous fun exploring all those dips and hollows, soft spots and firm skin over the past two weeks. They'd spent every spare second they could garner learning about each other's bodies. Stella was a dream come true.

Wyatt forced all those provocative thoughts away. It wasn't the right time. Later, he could think about what he'd like to do to Stella once they were alone.

Today had been one of the most difficult days of Wyatt's life.

Today was Bryce's funeral.

Levi and Cat had driven Stella and Wyatt to the Maplewood Cemetery, where the service and then internment of Bryce's ashes were to take place. Wyatt remembered little about the drive there, or about getting out of the car and walking to the allotted grassy area in the middle of the small cemetery. It was a blurry fog. The one thing he did remember was Stella's hand in his, leading him through the throng of locals gathered to pay their last respects, helping him take a seat in the back row of plastic chairs set up for the gathering.

Stella had been the one constant bright spark in the past few weeks, even as the guilt and shame sometimes threatened to overwhelm him. Whenever he delved too deep into the pit of self-recrimination, she was always there to pull him out of his funk.

He loved her so goddamn much, it hurt.

He'd held his breath before the sentiment swamped him completely and looked around for something to distract himself. At least it wasn't snowing for the funeral, but gunmetal gray clouds covered the sky, blocking out the view of the mountains; the temperature hovering near zero.

The rest of the Stargazer Ranch staff had come. Arrayed in the chairs on either side of him and Stella. Dean and Naomi had given him a solemn nod, as did Joseph, sitting beside them. Penny was next to Stella, offering her support in the form of a hand on her arm or a quick fix of a few wayward strands of hair that drifted down out of her bun. Dale and Steph, Gordon, Violet, Roxanne, and Janine were all there, too. Cat had told him they would all be here, to support Stella. But also, to offer him their solidarity. Looking at all the Stargazer squad arranged alongside him, a curious sensation settled in his chest. A sense of calm, as if all his burdens had suddenly become lighter. They accepted him for who he was, warts and all. It was a good feeling. Something like hope.

Sheriff Buchanan and his two deputies, Jude Wilder and Susan Nomad, caught his eye, standing at the back of the crowd, watching everyone with serious vigilance. There remained an edginess around the town, an aura of unease. And who could blame the locals, it wasn't every day four gangsters invaded the town and took two residents hostage, and hunted down two more, plus some stolen diamonds in the depths of the mountain range. Not to mention the FBI agents swarming all around the streets... Well, it'd take a long time for this kind of gossip to die down, if ever.

Wyatt flicked a look from beneath lowered eyebrows in Cat's direction. Her only consolation to the solemnity of the day was to swap her checked flannel shirt for a black turtleneck. Otherwise, she still wore her signature outfit of blue jeans, boots and her black biker jacket. Her blonde, spiked hair stood out as a beacon amongst the other mourner's dark hats and coats. The cast on her hand would remain for at least another four weeks. Which made Cat irritable and hard to live with, because she hated any sort of incapacitation; hated to feel powerless. Hated to have to ask Levi to open a jar of pickles for her. It also made her mechanic job on the ranch a little tricky, but ever-resourceful, Cat regaled them with stories of how she rigged up a vice system to help hold an engine part immobile while she worked on tightening a screw.

Both she and Levi continuously reminded him they didn't blame him for any of this, but it was hard not to feel a twist in his guts every time he saw Cat struggling to pull on her boots, or to cut up her dinner.

Levi sat on the other side of Cat, his bearded face grim and unsmiling. While he showed no outward signs of the ordeal they'd endured at the hands of Dmytro's thugs, Wyatt knew Levi still had bad dreams about the day Cat had been held hostage. Wyatt felt a surge of love for his kid brother. They'd had their differences growing up and Wyatt admitted he hadn't spent a lot of time in the house once their mother left, so he couldn't exactly say they were close. But they'd more than made up for that over the past six months, and now their brotherly bond ran deep.

Stella liked to say that everything happened for a reason, but Wyatt was still on the fence about that. At first, he'd been unable to see how Tony dragging him into this whole stolen diamond fiasco could be good for anyone. But then Stella reminded him, they wouldn't have spent a night snowbound in a truck without Tony's diamonds. And they certainly wouldn't have spent three horrific days in the mountains evading a hitman. It might've been ghastly, but it also brought them closer. After a lot of pondering, Wyatt conceded that perhaps Tony had brought him Stella together, after all.

Even so, he wasn't mourning Tony's death. Perhaps he should feel something, the guy had once been his friend. But he was still angry with Tony, especially for the way he'd given Dmytro's men Stella's name; he couldn't forgive him for dragging her into it.

Wyatt's sling had come off a week ago, but it still hurt to bend or twist; even laughing caused pain. At least he could drive his truck, now. Which meant he spent every available night out at Stargazer Ranch, waiting for Stella to finish her shift. Then he'd drive her back to his house, and they'd occupy each night cocooned in his bed, making love, until he drove her back again early the next morning. It wasn't an ideal situation, but it worked, for now. Soon, they'd need to sort something else out. Because the one thing he knew; he was never letting Stella go. She was his light and his reason for living.

CJ's had remained closed for the past weeks, no one sure if it were ever going to re-open. Wyatt needed to look for a new job, but he'd let his ribs heal for a few more weeks before he did that.

The service had been short, but surprisingly upbeat. The priest amused the crowd with exploits from Bryce's early days as a biker. Wyatt was shocked to hear Bryce had been married—his boss never mentioned anything about a spouse —but that his wife had died of cancer, which was what'd prompted Bryce to move to Stevensville and open CJ's. The initials stood for Crystal Jade, his wife's name, and she'd always dreamed of moving to Montana. Then the sound of heavy metal band Motorhead had rung out around the graveyard; Bryce's favorite song. A couple of Bryce's old mates from the biker gang stood up and began head-banging, making everyone laugh. Wyatt felt his shoulders relax. He'd been dreading this day, but even though people were sad at Bryce's passing, they were also glad to be able to celebrate his long, and mostly happy life.

As the service ended, Wyatt and the other three stood up and waited at the back of the crowd, watching as some went forward to talk to Bryce's family members. The rest of the Stargazer team milled around them, almost like a protective guard of honor. Surprisingly, most of the locals made an effort to drift in Wyatt's direction. Everyone liked Bryce, they all said. It was a shame to lose him. But they all gave him a brief nod, or a quick touch on the arm, as if to let him know they weren't blaming him. Not everyone did this, but enough to make Wyatt give a pensive smile.

A woman in her mid-fifties had come up and introduced herself to Wyatt just as everyone was leaving, telling him she was Bryce's sister. Before he had a chance to open his mouth and tell her how sorry he was, the priest had whisked her away to help him sort out some final arrangements.

Now, they were back at Levi and Cat's house, debriefing and unwinding after the tension of the funeral. Cat made them coffee and served up some peanut butter cookies Stella had made earlier. Wyatt removed his tie and had slipped a hoodie on over his head, but Stella was still wearing that provocative black dress.

There was a knock at the door. Wyatt was closest, so he jumped up to answer it.

It was the woman from the funeral, Bryce's sister standing on the doorstep. Without preamble, she asked if she could come in and talk to him. Wyatt squared his shoulders, bracing himself for her words of censure; God knew he deserved them. He could hardly look at her for the guilt that was eating through his stomach. Knowing she was going to blame him for her brother's death.

Wyatt directed her to the couch, and the sister settled herself in. He dared not take a seat himself and ignored the curious glances the other three were throwing at him. Stella stood and came over to take his hand in hers, broadcasting her subtle support.

"My name is Brianna," the lady said. Her intonation hinted that perhaps she'd spent a lot of time in New York. She was stylishly dressed in dark, tailored pants and a thick woolen coat that came to her knees, to ward off Montana's freezing conditions. Her perfectly coiffed hair was pulled back beneath an elegant black beret. "I'm Bryce's sister, as I already mentioned at the funeral. I'm also his closest living relative." At this she gave a wan smile. "We weren't that close, and I haven't seen a lot of my bother over the years." This much Wyatt knew to be true, as he'd never seen her visit Bryce and his boss had never talked about her. "But one thing I do know. He loved his burger joint. So, I have an offer for you. If you think you're up for it."

Wyatt's head sprang up. This wasn't what he'd been expecting at all.

* * *

Stella watched Wyatt close the front door behind Brianna, waving one last time as Bryce's sister walked back down the front path toward a waiting sedan. Wyatt joined them in the living room, and all four of them stood in stunned speechlessness.

"Wow, Wyatt. That's an amazing offer." Levi was the first to break the silence. "I think you should take it up, you'd be stupid not to."

Wyatt sat down next to Stella on the sofa, a dazed look on his face. "I need to think about it first," he replied. But Stella knew his brother was right, he would be foolish to say no. How could she convince him he was good enough to do this?

"I know what you're thinking," she said, scooting in next to him on the sofa so their knees were touching. "And you're wrong. You can do this. You should do this."

He stared at her and she stared back into his beautiful obsidian eyes, willing him to acknowledge her. Even though they'd only known each other for a short time, they had a sometimes-astonishing connection, almost as if she could drive straight to the heart of his misgivings, and he to hers. It was intense and a little scary, but in a good way. She knew he was scared he'd fuck this up, like he thought he'd done to the rest of his life. But along with Levi and Cat, she'd gently been spurring him on, helping him to believe he was worthy of a good life.

Bryce's sister's words still echoed in her mind. She'd offered Wyatt the head cook position at CJ's. She wanted to keep it going, to keep Bryce's legacy alive. Besides, the café had been making a tidy little profit, so Brianna was making a solid business decision. She'd heard good things about Wyatt, both from Bryce and from the locals in town. Over the past few days, she'd spent most of her time organizing the funeral, but had also asked questions, and mulled over the answers, finally coming up with a solution to her predicament.

"It's a big responsibility," Wyatt mumbled, standing and pacing around the room.

"Yes, it is," Cat agreed, entering the conversation. Stella glanced up at where she and Levi were standing close together behind the sofa. Wyatt shot Cat a look, as if he thought she might be mocking him. But there was a sense of purpose in Cat's gaze as she said, "And you'll never know whether you can handle it unless you take the job."

Stella cheered her on silently in her head. They might be hard words for Wyatt to hear, but Cat was doing the right thing. Wyatt needed to be challenged.

Wyatt stopped pacing to stare at her. Cat stared back, eyes flashing crystal blue as if laying down an ultimatum.

"It's time, Wyatt," his brother said. "Time to take that leap forward. We all have faith in you." Levi slipped his arm around his fianceé. "You can have what we have, if you've got the courage to take it."

Stella held her breath at Levi's words. It was almost as if he were daring Wyatt. Would it work?

It was her turn to up the ante. Stella stood and took a step toward him, close but not quite touching. "Will you do it?" she asked.

The whole room seemed to pause, waiting for Wyatt's answer.

"Yes. I'll do it."

As if released from a bowstring, Stella flung herself into his arms, careful not to hug him too tight because of his ribs. "That's fantastic," she gushed, kissing his cheeks, his forehead and finally claiming his mouth. "You'll be great." Her hands went around his neck and she reveled in the feel of his broad shoulders beneath her splayed fingers.

He could hardly get any words out, she was kissing him so soundly. Levi and Cat came and slapped him on the back, Cat even leaning in and giving him a quick peck on the cheek.

"Maybe you can have a go at some of your amazing recipes."

"Maybe," he laughed, trying to ward off her kisses long enough to grin at Cat and Levi. A cheerful grin, one full of promise for the future.

Everyone began talking at once, all expressing their pleasure and satisfaction at how the day had turned out.

This was such great news. And speaking of great news,

perhaps it was time to share her other announcement with Wyatt.

"I've got something good to tell you, as well," Stella said into the happy room.

The conversation died and three pairs of eyes turned to her, expectantly.

"I wasn't going to say anything until... Well, until after we got over the funeral. But Dean, my lovely, wonderful boss, mentioned that as part of the restoration on the ranch, he's commissioned three new cabins to be built up near Emily and Tom's cabin." She stopped to let her words take effect, but none of them seemed to get it. "Dean said I could have one." She clapped her hands with glee, unable to control her explosive feelings of joy. "*We* could have one,' she amended. "If we want it." The lightness in her chest ebbed away as a slight frown appeared on Wyatt's forehead. Didn't he want to move in with her? Oh God, had she misjudged him? Was this all happening too quickly? Had it been too soon after his offer by Bryce's sister?

"That's nice of him," Wyatt said a little too nonchalantly.

"What's the matter with you?" Cat demanded. "If it were me, I'd be jumping at the offer."

"I'm sorry," Stella stuttered, backing away from Wyatt, "It's too quick, isn't it? I didn't mean—"

"No. Stella, don't. It's not that I don't want to be with *you*," he blurted, finally understanding his blunder. "That's not what's worrying me," he added, taking her by the waist and dragging her in toward his chest. "I just don't want anybody to think I need a...handout. Just because I spent time in prison..."

And there it was, that chip on his shoulder about not needing help. He hated people to think less of him. He was so stubborn and so determined to do things his own way. But these traits were also some of the many things that drew her to him. His intentness, his stubborn will not to give in against any odds. It also made him a hero in her eyes. Stella realized it would take time and love to rid him of the bitterness entrenched in his soul at being treated so badly by the justice system. He had made huge leaps forward, and most of the time the old resentment had faded. But every now and then he needed to be reminded, he wasn't in this alone anymore.

She lifted an eyebrow. "It's not charity, Wyatt."

She stared at him, daring him to argue, locking her gaze with his.

Cat and Levi sidled quietly out of the room.

"Dean is doing this because he's a good man. And because he wants me to stay, and he also wants me to be happy. Maybe you could say it was an incentive for me to sign on for another year at the ranch. The builders will start next week, and they should be ready within a few months." Stella couldn't believe it. A place where she and Wyatt could live together."

"Hang on." Wyatt held up a hand. "You're staying for another year?"

She nodded. "At least." And who knew what would happen after that. She hoped she might stay indefinitely.

Stella hadn't mentioned that part to her mother, yet. Juliette was still getting over the shock of her daughter being involved in a diamond heist, even though Stella had played down her role as much as she could. She'd have to find the exact right opportunity to tell her mother. But there probably was no such time. Juliette would hate her decision, no matter what. She probably owed it to her mom to tell her face to face. She'd book a flight back to Lyon soon. Maybe she'd take Wyatt with her, that'd set the cat amongst the pigeons.

Stella had also talked to Aunty Celeste a few times over the past weeks. After her aunt had recovered from the shock of everything Stella had been through—Stella told her all the grim details, unlike her mother—her aunt mentioned she had a juicy bit of something to tell her regarding Armand. It seemed that Armand had moved on already. He'd started dating a woman he'd met while working out at the gym. Aunt Celeste wouldn't confirm it—she said she didn't stoop to that kind of gossip, and she wouldn't dream of hurting Stella with false rumors anyway—but Stella got the profound feeling that Armand had been seeing this woman for longer than the three weeks they'd been broken up. But she was in no position to throw stones. Look how quickly she'd fallen for Wyatt. Stella didn't begrudge Armand his happiness, she just wished he'd been more upfront about it, and not made her feel lower than dirt because she was the one who'd broken their engagement. But it'd been the right decision, in the end. Because look at what she'd found with Wyatt now.

"That's great." Wyatt's hesitant smile became one of elation. "You're staying," he repeated.

"I'm asking you to move in with me, Wyatt Wilson." She planted a kiss on his lips. They were warm and full of devotion. "We could spend every night together from now on. What do you say?"

He was her man. There was no other for her. She knew life with Wyatt wouldn't always be easy, but out here in the Big Sky Country there were so many possibilities. Her love for him could be as big as that sky above, if he let it. They had a chance at a future together and she wanted to grab it with both hands. But did he?

"Mm, when you put it that way," he growled playfully into her neck, pulling her up so he could kiss her. Her feet left the ground as he swung her gently around the room. "How can I refuse an offer like that?"

"Really?" She'd been hoping he'd agree, but there was still a nagging doubt he would see it as charity.

"Really," he said. "I love you, Stella. There's nowhere I'd

rather be. I'm sorry I didn't say yes straight away. I'm a bonehead and I apologize. If you'll have me, I'd love to share a house with you."

"Thank you." Sudden tears sprang to her eyes. It was another leap of faith by the man she loved, and she was so proud of him. Their love was going to get them through. This was just the start of a great love affair, and she couldn't wait to spend the journey with Wyatt at her side.

Want to know more about Stargazer Ranch?
Get your FREE and EXCLUSIVE Prequel Novella
STARDUST
Read Dean and Naomi's story.

GO TO THIS LINK FOR FREE COPY
dl.bookfunnel.com/mw5jp7zmaf

Stay in touch via my website
www.suzannecass.com

Facebook: www.facebook.com/suzannecassauthor/
Instagram: www.instagram.com/suzanne.cass/
Pintrest: www.pinterest.com.au/suzanne_cass/

If you liked Snowfall, then you might like the other books in the Stargazer Ranch Mystery Series.

Combustion - Prequel Novella

Wildfire - Book 1

Firelight - Book 2

Snowbound: A Christmas Novella Book 3

Cloudburst - Book 5

Also by Suzanne Cass
NEW
**Stormcloud Station Series
(A Stargazer Spinoff Series)
Small Town Romantic Suspense**
Clear Skies
Starlit Skies
Crystal Skies

**Stargazer Ranch Romance Series
Small Town Romantic Suspense
Combustion: Prequel Novella
Wildfire
Firelight
Snowbound: A Christmas Novella
Snowfall
Cloudburst**

**Island Bound Series
Mystery Romance (on an Island)**
Books can be read as stand-alone
**Bound by Truth
Bound by Silence
Bound by the Stars**

**Colors of the Earth Series
Small Town Romantic Suspense**
Books can be read as stand-alone
**Shadows in the Dust
Shadows in Deep Blue
Shadows of Red Earth**

Romantic Suspense
Single Title
Island Redemption

Glass Clouds
Chasing Bullets

Love in the Mountains Novella Series
Small Town Short Romance
Novellas can be read as stand-alone
Rain on a Tin Roof
Lost and Found
Rescue his Heart

Please Leave a Review

The greatest gift you could ever give an author is to leave a review. You will be helping other people to discover this book and making a difference to me as an Independently Published Author. If you liked this book and want other people to read it too, please leave a review.

About the Author

Suzanne Cass is an Australian author who writes rural romance and romantic suspense abounding with passion and danger.

Her debut novel, Island Redemption, won the Romance Writers of Australia Emerald Award in 2016. Suzanne was also a finalist in the 2019 Romance Writers of Australia RUBY award.

She had always had a fascination with the tough resilience of people who live in our amazing red-dirt outback country. When not writing about the characters that inhabit her head, Suzanne can be found roaming the Perth beaches with her border collie, or encouraging from the sidelines as her two sons play sport.

Visit her website www.suzannecass.com or subscribe to her newsletter via: www.suzannecass.com/contact

Acknowledgements

The stories keep on rolling through the Big Sky Country. Stargazer Ranch has become so much a part of me, I wish it were real some days.

Snowfall is the fifth novel in this series. I enjoyed writing Stella so much, as she is everything I would like to be. An accomplished pastry cook (Oh to be able to make those sweet treats set up behind the glass in just about every boulangerie in Paris) and unafraid to try anything. She certainly had the courage to conquer those mountains, even though she was a city girl at heart. And Wyatt holds a special place in my heart, he kept going, even after all the injustices he faced. I was so glad he found love with Stella. I spent a lot of my youth camping and hiking in the Australian mountains, but I still needed some guidance on the best way to survive the bitterly cold Bitterroot Mountains. My research took me deep into areas of survival I probably will never use, but were incredibly interesting, anyway.

Of course, this book wouldn't have been what it is today, without the help and guidance of my author tribe. Thank you from the bottom of my heart.

There is a team of people who I also couldn't do without, beta readers (big thanks to Rebecca, Jennifer, Dave and Ceara for their amazing feedback) and my ARC team, who are essential to an Indie Author like me, for their wonderful reviews. Big thanks to my editor, Tanya Saari

To my husband, Gary and to my two beautiful boys (who are turning into gorgeous men) Thank you for your unconditional love.

I am so very grateful to all the readers who have bought and enjoyed my books and who will continue to do so. Writing for you is what keeps me happy and contented. I hope you enjoy reading about the people who live on Stargazer Ranch as much as I'm enjoying writing about them.

www.ingramcontent.com/pod-product-compliance
Lightning Source LLC
Chambersburg PA
CBHW030428120726
47903CB00003B/855